Recycling
George

Recycling George

BY STEPHEN ROOS

Simon & Schuster Books for Young Readers

NEW YORK   LONDON   TORONTO   SYDNEY   SINGAPORE

SIMON & SCHUSTER BOOKS FOR YOUNG READERS
An imprint of Simon & Schuster Children's Publishing Division
1230 Avenue of the Americas, New York, New York 10020

SIMON & SCHUSTER BOOKS FOR YOUNG READERS
is a trademark of Simon & Schuster.

Book design by Anne Scotto
The text for this book is set in Bembo.
Printed in the United States of America
2 4 6 8 10 9 7 5 3 1

Library of Congress Cataloging-in-Publication Data
Roos, Stephen.
Recycling George / by Stephen Roos.
p. cm.
Summary: When twelve-year-old George's sister and brother-in-law move out of their trailer park while George is at school, leaving him behind, he moves in with a rich schoolmate and his family.
ISBN 0-689-83146-3
[1. Trailer camps—Fiction. 2. Wealth—Fiction. 3. Schools—Fiction. 4. Ohio—Fiction.] I. Title.
PZ7.R6753 RE 2002
[Fic]—dc21
2001020930

For David Wolfe

Recycling George

Chapter One

THE SCHOOL BUS is old. The windows are cracked.
Rust has broken out like acne on the chipped yellow
paint. Intricate webs of silver duct tape fail to conceal
the rips and cracks in the old vinyl seats.

The bus chugs along Mill Road. The rattles are
almost deafening. As Mr. Tiani downshifts for the
bridge the kids get a blast of the stink from the river
below.

"Yuck!"

"Puke!"

"Gross!"

Holding their noses, the kids leap out of their seats.
It takes only a second or two to slam all the windows
shut. It has to be the all-time worst smell in the world.
Rotten eggs, septic tanks, and the reptile house at the
Cleveland Zoo all rolled into one putrid odor. None

of the kids bother to look at the sickly yellow water below. Nor do they glance a few hundred yards up the river at the mill that is transforming a thousand gallons of clean water into poison every sixty seconds and layering the river with thick oily foam.

(The local environmental groups have tried to clean up the river forever. They've even sued the mill owners. The mill owners have sued them right back. Half the people in town work at the mill. No matter which way the court rules, it's going to be a big mess.)

A boy sits by himself, ignoring the rattles and the smell. Scrunched down in his seat with his knees pressed up against the back of the seat in front of him, he stares off into space.

His face is round, his eyes are wide set and friendly. Though no one ever says anything pro or con about his nose, the boy has recently decided that it's too big for his face. He likes his hair, though. It is black and hangs over his forehead, almost touching the thin metal frames of his glasses. He's overdue for a haircut.

The boy's name is George Honiker. He's twelve years old, and next month he's going to finish sixth grade at Bob Hope Middle. (The star grew up in Cleveland, but there's no proof he ever set foot in East Siena. It's kind of pathetic, but that's East Siena for you.) Today George is wearing a blue plaid flannel shirt, which is too warm for this time of year. He likes it buttoned all the way to the top, which makes it even warmer. The jeans are old. So are the sneakers. His big toe is coming through on the right sneaker.

(The shirt is too small for him too, but it's his favorite shirt. He got it for Christmas last year from his dad. His dad has been in the Florida Panhandle working on a ranch where they grow fat-free ostriches, so he doesn't know how much George has grown this year.)

The little smile on George's face turns into a grin. He scrounges around in his shirt pocket for a pencil. It's hardly two inches long, but if he wedges it between his thumb and the palm of his hand, he can get a decent grip on the thing.

He flips open the spiral notebook on his lap. It's his doodle pad. In big, thick lines he starts to draw pistons. Around the pistons he draws an engine. Around the engine he starts to draw the GTO he saw at the car show in Cleveland the month before.

The bus slows.

"Versailles Trailer Park!" Mr. Tiani shouts.

The brakes are noisier than the rattles. They don't stop screeching till the bus comes to a complete stop. George still doesn't hear them. He is too busy deciding if his GTO should have whitewalls or not.

"George!"

He feels someone behind him poking him in the shoulder. It's hardly more than a tap, but it startles him.

He turns abruptly. Fern Dachroeden is hovering over him, one hand in the air, looking like she's about to strike again.

"Hey, what was *that* for?" George complains. "I didn't do anything to you!"

"You live at the trailer park, don't you?" Fern Dachroeden asks.

"So what if I do?" he says. "You think it gives you the right to hit me?"

(Even if she is a public nuisance, George has to admit she's pretty enough in a girly-girl way. She even wears a little velvet headband with flowers embroidered on it.)

"Hit you?" Fern exclaims indignantly.

"You need to learn to keep your hands to yourself," George declares.

"I poked you, is all, you brat," she announces stiffly. "And that was just because you wouldn't listen when I tried to tell you it's your stop."

"My stop?" George asks incredulously.

"You're home, George!"

George looks out the window. There is no missing the massive gates at the entrance to the Versailles Trailer Park. "Oh, no!" George mumbles under his breath. As he springs out of his seat the spiral pad slips off his lap and into the aisle. He stoops to retrieve it, but Fern is too quick for him.

"Give it back!" George demands.

"Oh, George!" Fern teases, hugging the pad. "Can't I keep it? Please? Pretty please?"

As George makes one last futile grab for the doodle pad he sees Rennie Whitfield, a row behind Fern, jumping out of his seat. He's the richest kid in Miss Lemon's sixth grade. Blond hair in a preppy cut, big square face. Big square teeth, too. His shirt is the right size and he wears khakis.

"Give it back, Fern!" Rennie shouts.

"I just want to see what George is drawing!" Fern giggles as she sticks the pad into her book bag.

"But it's not yours!" Rennie protests, grabbing her bag.

George spots Mr. Tiani rampaging down the aisle. He's scary even when he's sitting in the driver's seat, but more so now as he plants one major (hairy) paw on Rennie's shoulder and the other (equally hairy) paw on the book bag.

"No picking on the girls, you guys," Mr. Tiani warns. "Not on my bus."

"But she stole George's pad!" Rennie protests. "She hit him too!"

"Oh, Mr. Tiani"—Fern pouts so prettily that George could hurl right on the spot—"make them stop picking on me!"

Mr. Tiani hands the book bag back to Fern. "Don't

you worry, honey," he tells Fern. "Those boys ought to be ashamed."

George knows a hopeless cause when he sees it. He scowls. "Oh, keep the doodle pad if you like it so much."

Eyes on the corrugated rubber floor, he runs down the aisle and jumps off the bus.

He's home.

(Well, it's home while George's father is in Florida. George's mom's been dead almost six years now, so he has no place to stay except with his sister and her husband, Karl, at the Versailles Trailer Park.)

It took a couple of months before George got used to living in a trailer. No matter if he lives there a hundred years, though, he'll never get used to the gates that lead into the park. Everyone in town makes fun of them. It's no wonder. They are almost fifteen feet high and their black vertical bars are capped with gold arrowheads. But the gates are plywood, not iron. They'd collapse if you tried to close them.

As parks go, this one isn't so big. Only thirty trailers are there now, plus concrete slabs with electric and water hookups (that means sewage, too) for five or six more. All the trailers are arranged in two rings around a humongous cement fountain. The splashing makes such a racket the residents took up a petition to get Mrs. Artoonian to turn it off.

(That will happen the year Hades freezes over. Mrs. Artoonian spent half her husband's life insurance on the fountain, and she means to get her money's worth. If Mrs. Artoonian had spent the money on some trees instead, the place might look halfway decent, George thinks.)

George follows the rest of the kids up the dirt road into the park. Some of their families are here for good. They've taken the wheels off the trailer, put down patio stones with a corrugated plastic awning over them. Some stay only a month or two. They move into regular houses or just another trailer park. George used to try to guess just by looks who was going in which direction, but he got it wrong so much of the time, he doesn't bother anymore. You never know.

George sees Lizard Artoonian up ahead. Her mom owns the park, so that makes her permanent. She's the shortest kid in sixth grade, and she's got pale skin and fine, curly hair that is so blond it might as well be white. Her eyeballs bulge out a little. It's probably her thyroid condition, but that's how Lizzie got to be Lizard. If she minds, she doesn't show it.

Sometimes when Lizard isn't looking, George draws doodles of her. Even if her hair and her skin and her eyes were normal, she'd still look weird. She always wears giant-size blue denim overalls and T-shirts she tie-dyes herself, plus lots and lots of thick plastic hoops around each wrist. Today they're all green. Tomorrow they'll be red or yellow or blue. The Rock and Roll Hall of Fame baseball cap she wears is permanent. For all George knows, Lizard sleeps with it on.

She's spotted something in the weeds at the side of the road. She scoops up a dented can that once contained Diet Dr Pepper. George doesn't know how she saw it. The grass is almost two feet tall.

"You going to get Fern Dachroeden, George?"

"Probably not," George says, sighing. "She didn't hit me all that hard, you know."

"She stole your doodle pad."

"It's just a dumb doodle pad. I got plenty more back in the trailer."

"Fern sure got Whitfield steamed," Lizard says. "Why would he want to do you any favors? It's not like you're friends or anything."

"Beats me," George laughs. "You wouldn't catch me jumping out of my seat if Fern stole *his* doodle pad."

"Or his ten-speed," Lizard adds. "Or one of his forty-six cashmere sweaters. Or his private jet."

"He doesn't have a private jet!" George protests.

"How do you know?"

"He's a kid," George says.

Lizard shrugs. "You want to go over to the recycling?" she asks.

George shakes his head. "Tammy's off soda. She says

it's bad for her digestion on account of her getting so pregnant."

Lizard shrugs again. Clearly she has very little patience for people who don't drink soda. "What are you going to do for money if you don't redeem some cans?"

"I'm getting money from my dad."

"The check that you were supposed to get last week?"

"You know how the mail is," George explains.

But Lizard isn't listening. She's found another empty. Classic Coke. She's got to have radar for empties, George figures.

Chapter Two

GEORGE'S DAD SENDS something to Karl and Tammy every month. That's for his clothes and food. When he can, he is supposed to send something extra to George direct. It's an allowance for treats like candy and movies and doodle pads.

Over the winter Mr. Honiker stopped sending it on a regular basis. When George spoke to him on the phone last week, though, his dad promised he'd put something in the mail first thing. It didn't come Tuesday or Wednesday, so George figures it's got to be here today.

Karl and Tammy's trailer is named Silver Bullet because that's how it looks. George has to squint on account of the glare from the sun on the shiny silver surface.

"Anybody home?" George calls as he steps inside. "George?"

"Yeah," he sighs, disappointed. "It's just me."

Everything is so *close*. The bathroom across from the door is too small for a bathtub, and the little bedroom at the back of the trailer has barely enough space for Tammy and Karl's bed.

Everything else is squeezed into the rest of the eight-by-twenty-foot space. Living, eating, TV. The couch folds out for George's bed at night. Everything else is built in. It's plastic, too. The little desk. The bureaus. Even the dining table is a plastic plank they pull out from the wall and prop up with detachable plastic legs when they sit down for a meal.

The TV hangs from a hook in the ceiling. It reminds George of his mom's hospital room. Tammy's watching it. She practically lives in front of the TV now. Eight months pregnant, and really big. By the time school gets out for the summer, George is going to have a little niece.

"What's happening?" he asks.

Tammy Anne aims the remote at the screen, turns down the volume. "Big typhoon coming," she says, eyes still on the screen. "They're calling up the National Guard."

"Here? You're kidding?"

"In Japan, silly. They don't get typhoons in Ohio."

"Well, you can always hope, can't you?" George asks with a shrug.

To save money, they dropped the cable. Now the only station that comes in is the Weather Channel. Karl brags that Tammy Anne knows more about what's happening weatherwise than anyone in East Siena.

"Where's Karl?"

"Over at the mill."

"Isn't he working graveyard?"

"Big meeting," Tammy says, still looking at the TV screen. "There's some pie on the counter if you're hungry."

George turns toward the kitchen area. All he sees are cereal boxes, cans of soup, chips and pretzels in cellophane bags, a stack of the bargain paper napkins that never stay on your lap. Under all that junk there's a counter, maybe even a stove and a sink.

On top of the coffeemaker is a pie tin. Empty. As George waves it in the air, the few remaining crumbs fall onto the electric green shag.

"Sorry," Tammy says. "I forgot I ate it."

"What kind was it?"

"Cherry."

"Oooh, my favorite," George says, trying not at all to hide his disappointment.

Sheepishly, Tammy shrugs. "There was this tidal wave in South America. I was so excited I couldn't help myself."

"Well, just as long as little Brittany enjoyed it," George announces ruefully.

"It's Danielle now," Tammy Anne tells him. "After the big hurricane last year."

"Why don't you just name the kid Hurricana, or Typhoona, or High Pressure Zona?"

Tammy Anne pats her belly gently. "How can you make jokes about your little niece?"

"The kid just got my favorite pie!"

At the end of the couch is a small two-drawer bureau. It's a built-in, of course. It's the only tidy spot in the entire trailer. If there's mail for him, Tammy leaves it there.

"The mail didn't come yet?"

"About an hour ago," she says, turning up the volume.

"Nothing for me?"

"You mean from Dad?"

George shrugs.

"I told you not to get your hopes up, George."

"It'll come," George assures her. "Tomorrow it will be here. For sure. He promised me."

George rifles through the top drawer of his two-drawer bureau. It's where he keeps his special things. The big manila envelope that's full of old family photographs is where it's supposed to be, but there are no doodle pads left. Darn it! Fern stole his last doodle pad.

Chapter Three

THIS MORNING IT'S on TV that the Ohio Supreme Court is about to make a decision about the mill. It's on every channel except the Weather Channel, so George doesn't hear about it till he gets to Bob Hope Middle. All the kids are yapping about what will happen if the mill closes down, when Miss Lemon comes in.

George likes her looks better than he likes her. Her hair is going gray and she doesn't wear any makeup. She kind of reminds George of his mom. Same blue eyes and the same smile. Once he even called her Mom by mistake. In class with everyone listening. It was very embarrassing.

The bell rings and the kids stand for the pledge of allegiance. Everyone sits down, except Fudge Sudow, two rows up. He's still standing and he's got his hand in the air too.

"What is it, Frederick?"

"Miss Lemon," he asks, "is the whole school going to close down?"

"Why on earth . . . ?"

While Miss Lemon shakes her head in confusion, some of the kids clap. The rest just laugh. Fudge is the class comedian. Every time he opens his mouth, everyone knows a joke is coming.

"The environmentalists could close down the mill, couldn't they?"

"Well, yes, but what's that got to do with us?"

"When they see all the toxins in our lunchroom, Bob Hope Middle is going to be history!" Fudge roars gleefully.

Some kids burst into loud applause. Some kids aren't even paying attention. Sallie Gardenia, last row, two aisles over, is reading a Bullwinkle comic book. Little Eddie Porter is sorting baseball cards. Miles Chen, right behind him, is passing a note to Weesie Knapp. Fern Dachroeden is thumbing through a notebook. At first George thinks it's his doodle pad, but it's too big and the cover is green, not black.

Lizard's one row down. She's wearing the bib overalls again, plus the red plastic bracelets today. When George sits up straight, he can see she's playing with her pocket calculator. Adding up her money, he figures.

"I guess our town would smell a lot nicer if the mill was gone," Miss Lemon tells Fudge.

Miss Lemon is very hip to the environment. The posters on every wall tell the story. Half of them show mountains, forests, and seashores so pristine they could be mouthwash ads. The other posters are smog-choked cities, rivers yellow from pollutants, garbage floating in an otherwise unsullied lake. Above the blackboard is the Indian with a tear coming down his cheek. Once George saw that one, he never threw a candy wrapper in the gutter ever again.

Rennie Whitfield, in the front row, is waving his hand like it's on fire. "The judge could make the company pay for cleaning up the river, too," he announces even before Miss Lemon calls on him.

Most of the kids clap, George included. He sees Lizard turning around in her seat, staring at him. She's shaking her head at him.

"What are you clapping for, George?" Lizard asks sourly in a very loud voice.

"The river stinks!" George explains. "You ever smell it?"

"But your sister's husband works at the mill, George!"

"So what?"

"So what's he going to do if the mill gets closed down?"

"Well, get another job, I guess," George tells her.

The kids are turning in their seats now, looking at him. It's worse than embarrassing. It's humiliating. George looks down at his desk, anything to avoid the busybodies' glances.

"Lots of folks work down at the mill," Lizard goes on. "Your dad, Molly. Your stepmom, Sallie. You guys are going to be in trouble if the mill closes. Doesn't anyone else get it?"

Even with his eyes still planted on his lap, George hears the chairs scraping on the linoleum. He's relieved the busybodies are checking out the other kids now.

"Well, that's something we need to talk about too," Miss Lemon says. "You are correct about that, Elizabeth. A lot of people could lose their jobs."

(Miss Lemon's brother has a secondhand-car lot out on Route 6. USED LEMONS is what the sign reads. A plastic lemon, eight feet wide and two feet high and as yellow as anything, is suspended above the sign. After the mill, it's the dumbest, ugliest eyesore in town. George wonders what Miss Lemon will say when the environmentalists go after her brother.)

"Well, there are other places to work, you know," Rennie says.

"Not around here," Lizard insists.

"But we have to take care of the environment," Rennie says.

"Aren't poor people part of the environment?" Lizard asks. "Isn't anyone supposed to take care of them, too?"

The class is quiet. No one has an answer for that. Not even Miss Lemon, and she's the teacher.

Chapter Four

WHEN THE CLASS breaks for recess, the sixth graders split up into two groups. The group around the jungle gym is kids whose folks work at the mill. The kids whose folks don't are hanging out around the old sandbox.

His father never worked at the mill, so George always used to hang out at the sandbox. When he moved in with Tammy Anne and Karl, he started hanging out at the jungle gym instead. It just happened. It's not something he thought about. Today he doesn't want to hang out with either group. Lizard is over at the swings. All by herself. George figures, why not?

When the board of ed turned the elementary school into a middle school, they left the playground equipment behind. Lizard's so short herself she doesn't look weird on little-kid swings. But when George sits down, his knees are way higher than his butt.

If he had his doodle pad, he could draw the utility shed on the other side of the baseball diamond. Or maybe the grandstand. Or maybe the Dumpster on the corner.

He notices Rennie Whitfield talking to some of the guys. Rennie looks up, their eyes meet. Rennie smiles, waves at him. Rennie breaks away from the guys, starts walking toward the swings.

He rests a hand on one of the gray pipes that holds up the whole contraption. "You get your doodle pad back, George?"

George shakes his head. "Oh, I don't think I'll ever see it again."

"It's not fair," Rennie tells him, shifting nervously from one foot to the other. "If she wants a doodle pad, she should pick on someone else."

"Got anyone in particular in mind?" George asks uncertainly.

"Someone who can afford it more," Rennie explains with a shrug.

George isn't sure if the put-down is intentional. Trust Lizard to make the most of it. "What makes you think George can't afford it?" she demands.

"I know you guys live down at the trailer park," Rennie says.

"Believe it or not, Whitfield, the folks down at the trailer park can afford all the doodle pads they want. We eat three times a day, too. In the winter we even have heat."

"Hey . . . I didn't mean . . . ," Rennie stammers.

George stiffens. "Come on, Lizard. Rennie's just being friendly."

"If he really wanted to be friendly, he'd ask you to his birthday party," Lizard announces.

George is embarrassed now. "Hey, what's that got to do with anything?" he asks Lizard.

"I heard him inviting Kyle Warnke on the bus yesterday," Lizard says, gleefully ignoring him. "It's tomorrow. After school. At the Whitfields' mansion. Isn't that right, Rennie?"

"Would you like to come?" Rennie asks George.

"Don't let her get to you," George says. "This is no big deal."

"I mean it, George. It's okay. I want you to come."

George shakes his head. He knows Rennie is just trying to be nice.

He waits till Rennie is safely out of earshot before he turns back to Lizard. "Did you have to be so obnoxious?" he asks her.

"You would have been just as obnoxious," she says, "if you'd heard Rennie telling Kyle about some glove he saw in the window down at Jack's Sports. I mean, he was practically telling Kyle what to get him for his birthday. That's how rich kids are. It's just so typical."

"Is Kyle getting him the glove?"

"What do you care?"

"Well, I don't," George assures her.

"It was so cool," Lizard chuckles. "Kyle told Rennie in no uncertain terms that he wasn't spending that kind of money on anyone but himself."

George puts a hand around each of the chains at the sides of his seat. One foot under the other, he pushes the swing back so far he's standing up again. Then he leans back into the seat and pushes with his legs. The seat goes halfway up to the crossbar at the top.

It's a risk. The swings were meant for little kids, after all. As George raises his legs, the swing goes into free fall. It lasts less than a nanosecond before the chains break. With a major *thud*, George plops onto the hard earth, the breath knocked out of him.

"Hey, you're not thinking about actually going to that dumb party, are you?" Lizard asks as she continues swinging away.

He's lying there, probably dying, but she doesn't seem to notice. He doesn't know how many bones are broken, but the pain is so intense, tears are coming to his eyes. "Are you kidding?" he gasps. "I wouldn't be caught dead there."

She sticks her feet out to the ground. As the swing

lurches to a stop Lizard turns to look down at him. If she's at all concerned that George is probably gasping his last, she's doing a good job at keeping it to herself.

"How does anyone get to be so insensitive as Whitfield, George?" she asks.

"Beats me," George gasps. "Maybe they take lessons."

Main Street is all Laundromats. There must be two to every block. People downtown live in small apartments. They don't have space for washers and dryers. Otherwise, it's bars, one pool hall, a health-food store, two coffee shops. A car wash takes up the whole block where Kriegel's department store used to be before it burned down.

Half the storefronts are boarded up permanently now. The asphalt is mostly potholes, and pretty soon the city will have to hire someone to mow the grass that's growing up through the cracks in the sidewalks. Hardly any traffic. Except for two teenage girls pushing baby carriages, and an old man standing outside a bar, George doesn't see any people. Most of the businesses that used to be downtown moved out to the malls years ago.

Big surprise why. As George nears the river the smell gets to him. Breathing through his mouth only makes it worse. Now he can taste it too. Just before the bridge George comes to the roller-skating rink. It's two stories tall with a flat roof. The windows are broken and the paint is peeling something fierce. The entrance has been boarded up, but the sign above it is intact. HONIKER'S ROLLER DERBY. George remembers the day his father nailed it up. There was a photo in the *East Siena Dispatch* the next morning.

If it weren't for Rollerblades, Honiker's Roller Derby would still be in business. Now just about everybody skates on the sidewalk. They don't have to pay to go to a roller rink. But George's father didn't know that Rollerblades were coming. How could he?

Just this side of the river is a little building, two stories high with a pitched roof and shingles on the sides that are painted bright blue. The building must have been a house once upon a time. Mr. Albion Jack still lives on the second floor, but the downstairs is now two plate glass windows with a glass door in between.

In one window is golf stuff; clubs, balls, tees, bags, gloves, hats, books are laid out on a green shag rug that's supposed to simulate grass. In the other window is stuff for all the other sports—tennis rackets, basketball nets, football helmets, a mountain bike. George spots the baseball gloves in the corner of the window. There are three of them. No prices.

(What the heck is he doing? He's not going to Rennie's party. And even if he were, he couldn't afford even a cheap mitt. But he can't help feeling curious as to what rich kids expect other kids to pay for their birthday presents. That's what he tells himself, anyway.)

George pushes on the door and steps cautiously into the store.

"Mr. Jack?"

No answer. As George closes the door behind him the water-stained floorboards creak beneath George's feet. Looking up, he sees that the only light is coming from a naked low-watt bulb dangling above the battle-ship gray metal shelves that line the walls.

"Anybody here?"

An old man shuffles out of the shadows. His glasses are slipping down his nose. The buttons of the old cardigan are in the wrong holes.

"Can I help you with something, boy?"

"It's George Honiker," George says firmly. "You remember me, don't you, Mr. Jack?"

The man steps closer, examines George's face criti-cally. "*The* George Honiker?" he asks. "The one and only George Honiker?"

George sighs. Old Mr. Jack remembers him, all right. He's just kidding around like always. "It's me, all right," George laughs. "The one and only."

"Nice to see you, George. What's the news from your dad?"

"Oh, great," George assures Mr. Jack. "Everything's going great for him down in Florida."

"Flamingo burgers, was it?"

"Ostrich," George says.

"Right," Mr. Jack says, making a face like he's about to throw up. "Knew it was something I couldn't wait to sink my dentures into. Your dad's something else. Always got some new scheme, doesn't he?"

George nods. He likes Mr. Jack because Mr. Jack likes his dad. As his eyes grow accustomed to the gloom he notices the odds and ends on the shelves.

"I saw some baseball gloves in the window."

"You like one of them, George?"

"Well, I'd like to look at one of them."

"Which one?"

"Outfielder's glove," George says.

Mr. Jack sets a cardboard box on the counter and extracts a glove. He holds it to his nose. Takes a whiff. "Quality leather," he informs George. "It even smells different."

He hands the glove to George. George takes a whiff for himself. Smells like the inside of the Mercedes at the auto show Karl took him to over the winter.

"You playing right field or left?"

"It makes a difference?"

"Just curious what position you're playing."

"I don't play," George says, shrugging. "It's for a friend."

"Wish I had a friend as generous as you are, George."

George doesn't get it. "Huh?"

"It's fifty bucks," Mr. Jack explains.

George shakes his head. He never imagined. "A little out of my league, I guess."

"Which league is that, George?"

"Huh?"

"American or National?"

This time George gets it. He fakes a smile.

"Next time you talk to your dad, tell him I asked after him, George."

"You bet," George says, stepping toward the door. "You think you could ever use some help running the store, Mr. Jack?"

"You looking for a job, George?"

"I was thinking my dad," George says. "When he comes back."

"Your dad's got bigger fish to fry than working in my store. I mean bigger flamingos to fry."

"Ostriches," George reminds Mr. Jack.

"Right," Mr. Jack says. "I'll remember that."

As George steps outside, the smell hits him full blast. "Damn river!" he exclaims as he crosses the bridge toward home.

Lizard's mom is dragging a lawn mower out of the

gray utility shed. The mower is so small George thinks at first it's a kid's toy.

Mrs. Artoonian is a real character. Lots of lipstick that makes her lips look an inch thick, plus eye shadow that's usually blue, but not always. Even to mow the grass, she's dressed up. Earrings and a necklace. A ruffled blouse and shorts printed with flowers all over. Her frizzy hair is hidden under a red-and-black-checked bandanna. She swears that when she gets around to writing up her memoirs, she's calling it *A Bad Hair Life*. She'll make so much money, she'll move to Arizona, she says. They don't have humidity there.

She tried to quit smoking over the winter with nicotine gum. Now she is addicted to both. She can chew and smoke at the same time, except when she's mowing. Leaning over the mower, she removes the wad of nicotine gum from her mouth and sticks it under the handlebar. She takes a serious drag from her cigarette and hands it to George.

"Here, George. Take it."

"What am I supposed to do with it, Mrs. Artoonian?"

"It's not safe smoking when you're mowing," she explains. "Remember that, George."

George drops the cigarette on the gravel, crushing it under his shoe.

"Hey!"

"It's not safe smoking even when you're not mowing," he explains as he sits on the lip of Mrs. Artoonian's fountain.

"You want something, George, or do you just like to watch old people sweating their buns off?"

George smiles. "Where did you get the cute little mower, Mrs. Artoonian?"

"The Siroccos left it. They don't have grass over at their new park."

"Why did they move?"

"Cheaper over there," Mrs. Artoonian sighs. "No fountains, you know. Some people just don't appreciate class, I guess."

Frowning, she reaches for the cord, gives it a tug. Nothing. The engine doesn't even begin to turn over.

"You check the gas?"

Shaking her head, Mrs. Artoonian unscrews the cap. "They left me an empty tank!" she exclaims. "The nerve of some people!"

"They're poor, aren't they?"

"That's no excuse," she exclaims as she reaches into her shiny gold fanny pack for another cigarette.

Chapter Five

THE PICKUP IS outside. Someone's home. As George steps inside the Silver Bullet he sees Karl in the doorway to the cubbyhole they call a bedroom, with a can of beer in his hand.

Karl is three years older than Tammy. He's too thin is the first thing you notice. The second thing is the Cleveland Indians baseball cap and all the curly red hair sticking out underneath. You can see his cheeks are pitted with little scars if you get too close. He must have had bad acne when he was a teenager. He wears jeans. Always wears denim shirts. He must have eight of them.

He's a decent enough guy. Took George to the auto show in Cleveland over the winter. Says he's going to take George to an Indians game this summer. Never complained once when George came to live with them.

"Where's Tammy?"

"Taking a nap," Karl says.

George nods. "I got invited to a birthday party," he says.

"Some kid here at the trailer park?"

"Some kid up in the Heights," George says.

Karl takes a swig of his beer. "How do you know someone there?"

"School," George explains. "He's in my class."

Karl sits on the yellow vinyl couch. George feels like Karl's invaded his space. It is George's bed, after all.

"I got to get him a present," George says. "If I go, I mean."

"Why wouldn't you go?"

"Well, it's not like we're that close."

"He likes you enough to invite you to his party," Karl says.

"I guess," George says.

"You like him enough to go?"

"Well, I never been inside someone rich's house," George admits.

"What kind of present are you thinking?"

"He's into baseball," George says. "I was thinking like maybe a baseball glove. They're not too cheap."

"How much, George?"

"Fifty?"

"You're asking me or telling me?"

"That's what they cost at Jack's Sports."

"Cheaper out at Wal-Mart."

"This kid wants the one at Jack's," George explains.

Karl takes a last swig of his beer. He crushes the can in one hand and tosses it across the room. It lands, miraculously, in the plastic trash can next to the kitchen counter.

"It's a lot for a kid's glove," he says. "We're kind of strapped, you know."

Karl turns to the bedroom. George's eyes follow. Tammy's up, wearing that red-and-yellow floral tent she calls a housecoat.

"Strapped? That's what you call it?" Without waiting for Karl to answer, she ambles out of the cubbyhole bedroom. The hair on one side is plastered to her head where she was sleeping on it. Without a glance at either George or Karl, she picks up the remote control, switches on the TV.

"He was just asking," Karl says softly.

Scowling, Tammy plops herself down in the straight-backed chair. "Between the baby and the environmentalists trying to close down the mill," she says, "we got enough to worry about."

"Look, I'm not sure I even want to go," George protests.

"Oh, you want to go," Tammy insists. "Why not admit it?"

George doesn't know what to say. He doesn't know what to think even. What's wrong with Tammy, anyway? "Since when am I not allowed to have any fun?" he asks. "Don't you want me to have friends?"

"Don't mind her," Karl says, taking a ten-dollar bill out of his wallet. "You get your friend a CD."

Tammy's out of the chair in a flash. Before George can take the ten bucks from Karl, she's grabbing it.

"Hey, what's that for?" Karl says.

"It's for the baby," Tammy tells him.

"Even with the baby we can manage ten bucks so George can buy his friend a present."

"Why?"

"Because he's your brother, that's why!"

"You didn't ask to be saddled with a twelve-year-old boy who eats us out of house and home, goes through clothes like a tornado."

"But you don't pay for any of that stuff," George points out. "Dad sends you a check every month for that stuff."

"Dad hasn't sent a check since Christmas," Tammy says angrily.

"No!" George protests. "He would have told me."

"Karl's been paying for everything, George. Grow up."

"But Dad's supposed to pay for my stuff!"

"There's a big difference between what Dad does and what he's supposed to do, George."

It's not the sort of thing anyone, even Tammy, would lie about. George knows that. Still, it takes a moment or two for the information to sink in.

"Karl?" George asks, but it's almost a whisper. "You been paying for everything for me?"

"Hey, it's no big deal, either," Karl says. "When your father gets back on his feet, he'll take care of things."

"I didn't know," George mumbles. "I just didn't know."

"Hey, it's not your fault," Karl assures him.

"But Tammy's right," George says. "You shouldn't be saddled with—"

"Hey, we're family, George," Karl says, pulling himself off the couch and coming to him. "No one's getting saddled with you, George."

But George can't bear it. He starts for the door.

"Hey, George," Karl says.

"Oh, let him go," Tammy says. "It's time he knew what was going on."

"Don't run away, George!"

Too late. George is already out of there. Slamming the door behind him, he pauses outside. Is he waiting for Karl to follow him? Is that what he's hoping for? He hears Tammy yelling at Karl. She's on a roll, madder at Karl now than she was at George. No way is Karl going to escape from that.

As George catches his breath he breathes in the sweet, green earth smell of grass that's just been cut. The mower's gone now. So is Mrs. Artoonian. But he can hear the *clink, clink, clink* of aluminum cans rustling against one another.

He sees Lizard coming toward him, wheeling her old, loopy-wheeled shopping cart full of empty cans.

"You want to go over to the recycling with me?"

"Maybe," he says. "I don't know."

"Well, make up your mind."

"How many cans do you need to make fifty bucks?"

Lizard scrunches up her lips now. "What do you need fifty bucks for, George?"

"Oh, nothing," George says.

Chapter Six

IT'S PROBABLY NOT in the rules, but it may as well be. Boys eat with boys, and girls eat with girls. The only exception is Norman Kremitz. He started eating with the girls back in third grade when the boys teased him about his paper dolls. Even though he gave up the paper dolls the next year, he still sits with the girls.

Today the topic at the boys' table is sneakers. Fudge Sudow has just announced that his brother spent more than a hundred bucks for a pair of Nikes.

"It's stupid," Dik Kenneally says. "No one should spend that much."

"Rennie's got Nikes," Fudge says. "More than one pair, don't you, Rennie?"

"I guess." Rennie takes a noncommittal bite of his sandwich.

"You're not sure how many pairs of sneakers you have?" Fudge teases. "Like anyone could believe that."

It's not the first time the conversation at the boys' table has got around to how much money Rennie's family has. Even if George can't feel sorry for Rennie or his money, it's cool the way Rennie doesn't take the bait. *Did someone teach him that?* George wonders.

Rennie shrugs good-naturedly. "Your brother a runner, Fudge?"

"Nah," Fudge says. "He's just trying to impress some girl."

"Like you're trying to impress us, Fudge?" Rennie asks.

The boys burst out laughing. For once the joke's on Fudge. He tries to laugh along with the kids, but George sees his face turning beet red.

"Guess someone got you finally!" Bobby Driscoe says gleefully.

"Oh, shut up," Fudge says. "So my brother bought a pair of running shoes. What's the big deal!"

The warning bell rings. George sees the girls stand up, arranging the garbage neatly on their trays. *Why do girls do that?* he wonders. *What's wrong with them, anyway? It's garbage! Don't they get it?*

Normally he lingers behind with the boys, but today he's in a hurry. He runs to the head of the line, drops the paper in one garbage can, the soda can in the other. He rests the tray on the stack and darts out into the hall.

Except for Mrs. Haley posting notices on the bulletin board, the hall is empty. The walls are old brown tile. It's more like the lavatories on the interstate than a school. George's sneakers squeak on the just-polished brown linoleum as he breaks into a run. If he hurries, he can make the call before he has to be back in class.

"No running, George!"

"Yes, Mrs. Haley," George mutters, slowing down till he's past her.

The pay phone is just on the other side of the principal's office. It's not the most private place in the world to make a call, but what can George do? He couldn't call from the trailer, and the pay phone outside Mrs. Artoonian's office was broken.

He sticks his hand in his pocket. He scoops out a handful of quarters. He's got a dozen. He hopes it's enough. How much can it cost to call Florida, anyway? He picks up the receiver, listens for the dial tone. He punches in the numbers. He knows them by heart now. Once a week, on Sunday morning, he calls his dad. This is the first time he's ever called when it wasn't Sunday.

"That will be a dollar seventy-five for the first three minutes."

"Okay," he says. "I got it. Just give me a second."

What a jerk! He's talking to a recording!

One, two, three. By mistake he drops the next quarter. It rolls along the linoleum. Doesn't matter. George isn't about to go running after it. Four, five, six, seven. He waits impatiently for the phone to ring at the other end. When it does, he starts to count. One ring, two rings, three rings. It's noon. Probably his dad's not even home.

"Be home," he whispers into the receiver. "Be home. Please."

The receiver still plastered against his ear, he feels someone tapping him on the shoulder. He spins around on his heel. It's Whitfield. George shakes his head. Whitfield holds a quarter between his thumb and his index finger.

Smiling, George takes it, stuffs it into his pocket. He mouths, "Thanks," but Whitfield isn't going anywhere. He's just standing there.

The phone keeps ringing. How's George supposed to talk to his dad with Rennie hanging around? He's almost relieved that his father isn't picking up.

"No one home, I guess," he says to Rennie. George hangs up the phone and collects the seven quarters the machine owes him.

The bell rings. The boys start walking back to Miss Lemon's classroom.

"You remember about my birthday?"

"I'd like to come," George says. "I don't think I can make it."

"Hey, I know Lizard can't stand my guts," Rennie says. "That doesn't necessarily mean you hate me too, does it?"

"Well, not necessarily," George says.

To George's surprise, Rennie grins. "You're okay, George," he says. "I knew I liked you."

Right away George wants to ask Rennie why he likes him, but only a nerd like Norman Kremitz would dare to ask something that weird. Mostly, though, he's just happy that Rennie really likes him. "You're okay too, Rennie," George says. "I like you."

"That's what I thought all along," Rennie says cheerfully.

They are friends now. It's official. George is glad about it too. Rennie is a decent kid, no matter what Lizard says. Probably if Rennie weren't rich, they'd have become friends earlier on.

Chapter Seven

GEORGE GETS BACK to his seat just in time. When the bell rings, Miss Lemon starts in about the arts fair coming up the last week of school. She doesn't get very far before there's a knock at the door. It's Mrs. Haley, from the principal's office. She whispers something to Miss Lemon. They both go out in the hall.

The kids look at one another, start to whisper.

Miss Lemon comes back in and taps on her desk with her knuckles. "Quiet, class. Frederick? Will you go with Mrs. Haley? Take your things too."

"Schoolbooks, too?" Fudge asks.

"Leave the school things," Miss Lemon says. "Just take all your personal things."

"Whatever they told you," Fudge says, laughing, "I didn't do it."

The kids laugh, but it's nervous laughter.

"No one's in trouble," Miss Lemon assures them. "Your parents will explain."

"My parents?" Fudge asks as he crams his pencils and notebooks into his book bag.

"They're outside," Miss Lemon says, folding her hands nervously.

It's very quiet. When Fudge is ready, Mrs. Haley leads him out of the classroom. All the kids are looking at him. He doesn't look back once. He's really upset, George can tell.

"What's going on?" Dik Kenneally asks. "Did someone die or something?"

"It's the mill," Miss Lemon explains. "The court has shut it down. Frederick's parents have to move."

"Just like that?" Weesie Knapp asks.

"Just like that," Miss Lemon explains.

Chapter Eight

BEFORE, THEY COULDN'T stop talking about the mill. Now that it's happened, no one talks at all. As the bus chugs through town it's strangely quiet inside. No one's even whispering. When the bus crosses the river, no one jumps out of their seat to slam the window shut. No one even groans about the smell.

The stink is still there, all right. Even if you hold your nose, the stink permeates every pore. How long does it take for a smell like that to go away? A day? A week? Who knows? But now that the mill is shut down, it's only a matter of time.

The bus slows down at the Versailles Trailer Park. George stands up, follows the other kids off the bus. He doesn't hear one "trailer trash" peep. Even the snobs know there are times you can't make fun.

He follows Lizard past the gates. It's an overcast day,

but it's hot. It's only when he's inside the park that he realizes not so many kids got off the bus as usual. Debbie Banacek isn't with them. Neither are the second graders whose names he never knew. He's about to ask Lizard about them, but she's checking the grass at the side of the road. He waits for her to swoop down on some empty, the same way gulls prey on fish in Lake Erie, but when she looks up, she hasn't got a can in either hand. She just looks straight ahead, her face all scrunched up.

"What's wrong?" he asks. "You step on something?"

"It's the Weisheits' trailer," she says.

George follows her eyes along the road to the first row of trailers. All he sees is an empty cement pad where the Weisheits' trailer used to be.

"So they moved," George says, sighing.

"It's not the only empty pad," Lizard says cautiously. "Look, George. It's not just the Weisheits' trailer. The Gordons' trailer is gone. So is Mr. Zaks's. They're all gone, George."

It's true. As he looks around he sees trailers missing all over the place. George breaks into a run. As fast as he can, he's running to the back of the park.

"Where are you going, George?" Lizard yells.

"I got to see," he gasps, though he doesn't say what it is he's got to see. He doesn't have to. Frantic now, he runs to the second ring, turns right. Thirty feet down he comes to a sudden stop. One, two, three trailers in. Where the Silver Bullet should be, there's only another empty cement pad.

He hears Lizard's footsteps, running up behind him.

"Someone took the Silver Bullet," he gasps. "It's gone! The Silver Bullet's gone, Lizard!"

He hears a door slam. "George!"

He spins around on his heel. Mrs. Artoonian is coming across the lawn. In one hand she has her usual cigarette. In the other, an envelope.

"It's going to be okay, George," she assures him. "You don't have anything to worry about. Everything's going to be okay."

If Mrs. Artoonian gets any more reassuring, George is going to have a total breakdown. "Where did they go?" he asks frantically.

She hands him an envelope. GEORGE is written in big block letters. Yellow marker.

"What happened?" George asks.

"Read the letter, George," Mrs. Artoonian commands.

Hands trembling, he tears open the envelope. Inside there's a single sheet of lined paper with three holes on one side. The writing is in the same yellow block letters. It's Tammy's handwriting, of course. She never did get the hang of writing cursive.

• • •

George,
We had to go north. Karl got offered another job, but if he isn't there by noon, he'll lose it. I didn't want to leave like this, but what with the baby, you know. You can stay with the Artoonians for a while. It's okay. I checked. In a couple days, when you're ready, you come up to Pittsfield.

Enclosed is $50 for the bus. You're not a bad kid, George. You just don't know what real life is all about yet.

Tammy

The bills are attached to the top of the page with plastic paper clips. George counts them out, four tens and two fives. He's never had so much money before.

"They couldn't stop by the school?" he asks, tears coming to his eyes. He doesn't care. He wants Mrs. Artoonian and Lizard to see how he feels.

"They didn't have time, George."

"It's, like, ten minutes," he shouts angrily. "They didn't have enough time for that?"

"I got all your clothes," Mrs. Artoonian says, patting his arm. "Your sister brought them over before they left. You stay as long as you want."

"It wasn't Karl. It was Tammy," he gasps. "She just ran out on me, didn't she?"

"No one ran out on anyone," Mrs. Artoonian says as she wraps an arm around George's shoulder and pulls him close.

He resists. No one can make him feel better now. It would be better if no one even tried. He's just got to feel really scared now, is all.

"It was crazy around here, George," she explains. "One minute, everyone's all upset about the mill, asking how they're going to pay their rent here. The next minute, they hear about the jobs up in Pittsfield. Half an hour later half the trailers are gone. Didn't even pick up their deposits they were in so much of a hurry. Come inside and I'll fix you a peanut butter and baloney sandwich, George."

"I don't want anything to eat," George protests.

"You'll feel better when you eat something," she assures him.

His face is getting red again. The tears are back. "I'm not hungry, Mrs. Artoonian," he insists. "I told you already!"

"Doesn't matter," Mrs. Artoonian announces. "You eat something, you'll feel better. You got something better to do?"

But he doesn't hear a word Mrs. Artoonian has said. "It's Tammy," he says. "It's all her fault. If she thinks I don't know about real life. . . . Running out on me like that. I'm not taking it anymore."

"Like you got a choice?" Lizard asks.

George takes a deep breath. How did the fear turn to anger so fast? All he knows is if he's got a choice, he'll take mad over scared any day. Right now he'd like nothing better than to rip the fifty dollars into shreds. But even as mad as he is, he knows that won't do anyone any good. He sees his bike leaning against the utility shed. Stuffing the money in his pocket, he heads for it.

"Where are you going, George?" Mrs. Artoonian asks.

"I'll be back. Don't worry."

He gets on the bike, rides it down the dirt road, past the gates. When he stops at the street, he hears Lizard running after him. Before the light changes, she's caught up with him.

"You're going to spend that money on a present for Rennie Whitfield, aren't you?" she asks, panting heavily.

"None of your business," he exclaims.

Finally the light turns. He's so anxious to get away from her, he stands on the pedals to make his getaway.

Chapter Nine

THE PACKAGE IS wrapped in green-and-yellow paper with blue ribbon. It bounces in the wicker basket that hangs from the handlebars as George rides his bike up Heights Road. The Whitfields' mansion must be three miles from town. The last mile is mostly uphill, too. By the time he gets there, he's sweating hard.

The driveway is crushed stones. All white. It looks more like carpeting than gravel. It's a long driveway. Two or three hundred yards maybe. On one side is an orchard. The trees, George isn't sure what kind, are covered with pink and white blossoms. Apple maybe. Cherry. On the other is a meadow, where an old horse grazes on spring grass.

A breeze comes up, freeing the blossoms from the stubby branches of the fruit trees. As they swirl around his head he closes his eyes. It's like being lost in a TV commercial for fabric softener. George waits till the breeze dies down before he opens his eyes again.

The Whitfields' house stands imposingly at the end of the driveway. It's stone too, but gray. Fieldstone, it's called. The gloss on the dark green shutters makes them shine in the afternoon sun. The trim is white. The house is three stories tall. Plus there's a garage with doors for four cars. If it had a moat and some turrets, George thinks, some royal person could move right in.

George hears kids laughing somewhere. Rennie's party, obviously. For a moment he feels afraid. What's he doing here? he wonders. If his rotten sister hadn't been so against it, if she hadn't ditched him too, would he even have bothered?

George fumbles for the brass knocker. His left sneaker catches on the doormat. He trips forward into the door. It gives, and George goes into free fall. A split second later he's sprawled on the black-and-white-checkered floor of the Whitfields' center hall, still hugging Rennie's present to his chest.

He isn't hurt, but the cold floor feels good on his hot, sweaty back. It's not linoleum, like he thought it was. It's marble. Slowly he sits up and looks around him. Through the glass doors to the left George can see a dining room. Behind him a thickly carpeted staircase spirals to the second floor.

"Anybody home?"

Of course no one hears him. How could they? He's whispering, which is idiotic, but what kind of person could shout in a place like this? It's more like a museum or a library than somebody's home.

George gets to his feet. He peers into the dining room. The walls are painted white halfway up. The rest is striped wallpaper to the ceiling. A massive, oval-shaped mahogany table stands at the center. Around the table are twelve large chairs, but the table is so big, you could add twice as many and everyone would have plenty of room. Above the table is a chandelier. Real candles in it too. Must be fifty of them.

George walks across the hall. The living room is even bigger than the dining room. A flagstone fireplace takes up almost all of the far wall. Above it is an oil portrait of a young woman, with very dark eyebrows and very, very white skin, in a pink ball gown.

George steps inside. Facing each other from opposite sides of the fireplace are two dark brown leather couches. Armchairs are clustered around a table at the near end. There's no television, but George knows the Whitfields have got to have one. Probably state of the art, too. It must be in another room somewhere. No built-ins here, George notes. If you live in a mansion, you have space to spare.

At first he thinks the living room is empty too.

Then he spots two people huddled silently over a table at the far end. As George steps closer he realizes they are playing chess. One of them is an old woman. The other is a girl. Not a kid. Probably college age. She turns toward him, smiles, but she doesn't say anything before turning her attention back to the chessboard. Her auburn hair is gathered in a low ponytail. She's wearing a blue-and-white-striped shirt and brown riding pants. She's even wearing boots, George sees.

"Hello, young man. How'd you get in here?" the old woman asks, still not looking up from the chess game. "The party's not in here, you know."

Her skin is so white, it looks like she never went out in the sun. Her hair, held in place by a tortoiseshell headband, is so white that it almost matches her skin. Everything else about her is pale blue—her eyes, her blouse, her skirt, her shoes.

George shrugs. "The front door was open. I was going to knock, honest, I was."

"So you just walked right on in, did you?"

"You should lock it, or someone could come and steal your stuff."

"Well, see anything around here you'd like to steal?" she asks, her eyes still on the board.

"Not yet," George admits.

The woman moves the knight. "Aha!" she exclaims, clearly delighted, as she takes one of the girl's pawns.

"If you'd moved the other knight, you could have checkmated," George says.

The woman frowns, glances up at George for the first time. She sits back in her chair as she looks him up and down slowly. George shifts nervously from one foot to the other.

"You play?" she asks.

"Used to," George says. With his dad, but he's not going to mention that to a stranger.

"So there's nothing you want to steal," she asks. "Is there something wrong with our stuff?"

"Nothing," George exclaims. "Honest. I just don't steal other people's things."

"Don't mind Ga," the girl says, smiling. "She's not usually such an awful old crab."

"Who could blame me?" the old woman protests. "The boy hates the way I play chess as much as he hates my taste! In my day, boys introduced themselves before they went in for the insults."

"You haven't given him a chance to introduce himself, Ga!"

"Perhaps he doesn't have a name!" The old woman raises her eyebrows. "Is that the case, boy? No one bothered to give you a name?"

"It's George."

"George what?"

"George Honiker."

"Hello, George," the old woman says. "I have a name too. It's Mrs. Whitfield. My chess opponent, the lovely thing I was beating at the game—without your help, I might add—is Brett."

"Hi, George," the girl says.

"She's Rennie's sister. I'm just the grandmother," the old lady says. Her glance falls on the package in George's hands. "You're late, you know. The other boys got here an hour ago."

George nods. "I'm sorry. I just—"

"You don't need to explain," the old lady says. "The party's down at the boathouse. Just go through those doors and down the hill. The boys should be back from their boat ride soon enough."

"Well, thanks."

"Unless you'd prefer to stay up here with us," the old lady says.

"Well, it's not like I wouldn't like to."

"Oh, don't try to get on my good side now," the old lady says with a dismissive wave of the hand. "It's too late for that, young Mr. Honiker."

The French doors open onto a flagstone terrace. It's covered with elegant wrought-iron chairs and a table with an umbrella growing out of the middle of it. It has green and white stripes, just like the cushions on the chairs. Getting things to match like that has got to be one of the best things about being rich, George figures.

He turns back to the house.

"Ma'am?" he asks the old woman.

"What is it, George?"

"The girl in the picture in the pink dress," he says. "Is that you?"

"My, oh my, aren't you the observant one," she says. "Go to the party, George. If you don't hurry, there won't be any cake left."

Nodding, George crosses the flagstone terrace. All around it flowers are planted neatly in beds. No fountains, though. George can't wait till Mrs. Artoonian learns she has a fountain and the Whitfields don't. Three hundred yards below he sees the river. At the river's edge—half on land, half in the water—stands the boathouse. Made of fieldstone too, it's like a miniature of the Whitfields' main house.

The door is open. As George steps inside he sees that the first floor *is* the pier. Two boats, one a small cabin cruiser, the other a sailboat, are moored at slips inside. At the far end are three openings the same size and shape as the openings for cars in a garage.

George sees the stairway. Quickly he climbs up to the second floor. It's one big room with lots of wicker furniture all over the place. A row of windows looks out over the river. Under the windows is a long table with a cake on it and a lot of presents, all of them opened.

He looks out the window. It's the same river that

flows through the town, but up here the water is clear. He can see the reflections of the sun, the trees, even the boathouse itself, in the water. He takes a deep breath. How long has it been since he has seen a river that doesn't stink? he wonders.

He hears someone coming up the stairs. It's Brett.

"They're not hiding, in case you were worried," she says. "They're just out on the river. Ga gave Rennie a boat for his birthday. He's out showing it off to the other kids. They'll be back soon enough."

"That's okay," he assures her. "It's nice looking out at the river." He takes another deep breath. Through his nose, too. "Wish it smelled as nice downtown."

"It will," Brett says. "Now that we got the court to rule against the mill."

" 'We'?"

"Well, some committees I'm on."

"So you're the one to blame?"

"Blame me for getting our river back?" she laughs, throwing her head back. "Aren't congratulations in order?"

"For closing the mill, I mean."

"Well, it was about time," Brett says. "They had no right polluting the river like that."

"My sister's husband worked at the mill," George says. "Now we got to move."

"Move?" Brett asks. "Why on earth?"

"For work," George explains. "My sister and her husband moved already. I got to go tomorrow."

"You don't live with your parents?"

George shakes his head, but he doesn't explain. He doesn't have to. He doesn't know this girl.

The girl nods. "How can anyone move that fast?"

"You can if you live in a trailer."

"Don't you go to school?" Brett protests. "Couldn't your family wait till summer vacation? It's only a month away, you know."

"It's paycheck to paycheck down at the mill," George says. "My sister's going to have a baby, too."

Brett shakes her head. Her shoulders sag. For a moment she's very still. She's got it. Finally. "I'm sorry," she says so softly it's like she's suddenly lost her breath. "All I thought about was the river. What a jerk I am. I never thought about . . ." She fidgets with her hands. Her voice cracks. She's upset. George can see that plainly.

"It's okay," George says, trying to reassure her.

"No, it isn't," Brett says emphatically. "It's not at all okay. You shouldn't have to move so abruptly. You shouldn't have to move at all if you don't want to."

"It's not like I have much choice," he points out.

"Well, you should," she says. "It's not fair. If you feel like staying till the end of the school year, you should be able to do it."

"Where would I live?"

"Don't you have friends?"

"No one I can just move in on for a month!"

She thinks for a moment. "Stay here, why don't you? We've got all this space going to waste."

"That's dumb," George says. "You don't even know me. Besides, my sister's expecting me."

"But there's got to be something," Brett insists.

"Like what?"

"I don't know," she says. "I just wish . . ."

"Me too," George says.

She nods sadly, helplessly. Without a word she starts back down the stairs.

When he hears the door downstairs slam, he turns back to the river. Even before he sees Rennie's boat, he hears the engine. The boat comes into view now as it skims across the water, glistening white in the afternoon sun. It's about twenty feet long. On the other side of the windshield George sees Rennie at the wheel. Dik Kenneally is in the passenger seat next to Rennie. Squeezed in behind are five other guys George recognizes from school. They're not all rich, George knows. But none of their families is poor. George is the only kid from the Versailles.

George takes a look at the presents Rennie has received. A shirt. A sweater. The other three presents are baseball gloves. George can hardly believe it.

Counting the one George brought, that makes four. As he checks them out one by one he sees they are better quality than the mitt he bought at Mr. Jack's.

The motorboat disappears into the boathouse. *It's okay*, he thinks. *No one's looking.* With all his might he hurls his package out into the river.

Chapter Ten

THE KIDS STOMP up the stairs to the second floor of the boathouse. They all act like they are glad to see George. They even say they are sorry he didn't get there early enough for the ride in Rennie's new boat. It doesn't seem to matter that he doesn't have a present. If anyone noticed, they don't say anything about it. *They're nice kids,* George decides. *It's not their fault they got money.*

When George gets back to the Versailles Trailer Park, it's almost dark. Mrs. Artoonian is out by her fountain chatting with some of the other ladies. On the ground, at her feet, is a black plastic garbage bag. Spilling out of it are the plastic flowers she plants every spring.

"I got the bus schedule, George," she says. "They got a Trailways every three hours to Pittsfield."

"Thanks, Mrs. Artoonian." Without looking at it, George stuffs the schedule into his pocket.

"You could plant real flowers," he tells her. "The soil looks good enough."

Taking a long, deep drag from her current cigarette, she holds a lavender tulip out for George. "You tell me, where am I going to find anything real this pretty?" she asks. "Besides, the real ones die back by the time spring is over. These last all summer."

"But the colors don't look real. They're all faded."

"I like them all pale," Mrs. Artoonian says cheerfully. "I think they're prettier. I've had these tulips since before Lizzie was born! Can you imagine!"

George steps inside the Artoonians' trailer. It's bigger than the Silver Bullet, but it's even more cramped. The main living area is all junk. Half the stuff comes from the town dump. The other half is going there. No one but Lizard and her mom know which is which, but there's not one place for anyone to sit.

It's got two bedrooms, too. Lizard's has bunk beds. Even so, it's funny sharing a room with her. He wonders why she doesn't move into the other room for the night. Wouldn't she rather sleep with her mom? If there were a couch or even an easy chair, he'd volunteer for that.

Lizard is stretched out on the bottom bunk. She's wearing a sweatshirt and sweatpants, but the plastic hoops are still up and down both arms. The Rock and Roll Hall of Fame cap, however, is on the little table next to her bed. So she doesn't sleep in it after all.

There's a paperback that's propped up on her stomach. This one's called *Unbridled Passions.* One of those dumb romance stories she's always reading. There's a castle on the cover, with a lady on a horse in front.

"Nice party?" she asks. Her eyes are still fixed on the book, but she isn't reading, just pretending. George knows it's just to make sure he knows she's still mad at him.

"It was okay."

"Did Rennie like the mitt?"

George shrugs. "How did you know I was going to buy it?"

"I know you, George. I saw how mad you were at your sister." Lizard looks up at him. "So, how did your gift go over with the rich kid?"

George shrugs again.

"He didn't like it, did he?" she exclaims indignantly. She closes her book, sits up suddenly. "I knew he was a pig. Typical. Typical."

"It's no big deal, Lizard," he says, scowling.

"But you spent fifty dollars on it? Didn't he even say thanks? What kind of a creep is he, anyway? Even for a rich kid, he's—"

"Give it a rest, will you?"

"Huh?"

"I didn't give him the mitt," George says. "I decided not to. You happy now?"

"You didn't buy it, George?" she asks.

"Oh, I got the mitt, all right," George assures her sadly. "I just didn't give it to him, is all."

"You going to take it back to Mr. Jack tomorrow and get your money back?"

"Can't," George says, shaking his head.

"Can't?"

"I tossed it in the river," he says.

"You what?"

"Three other kids gave him mitts," George explains. "Better quality, too. I wasn't going to give him junk."

"You're a jerk!" Lizard exclaims. "You're a total jerk, George. You're the worst jerk I ever met."

George hoists himself into the upper bunk. His blue pajamas are in one of the shopping bags that Tammy left, but he's not about to change into them with a girl around. Even Lizard.

He unzips one of the duffel bags, scrounges around till he finds the big manila envelope with all the family photos inside. He doesn't open it. He just needs to know it's there.

"So how are you supposed to get to Pittsfield tomorrow without any money?" Lizard asks.

"I'll have to worry about that tomorrow, I guess."

"Better not ask your sister for more," Lizard warns. "If she found out, she'd skin you alive!"

"Sounds like something she'd do," George says. He turns out the little light on the wall.

Lizard turns out her light too.

"You got to get the money somewhere, George."

"I'm asleep, Lizard."

She turns on her light anyway. "I got almost fifty bucks from the recycling. I've been saving it for a rainy day."

"I couldn't pay you back," he says.

"It's not a loan," she says.

"Oh."

He sits up in bed, swings his legs over the side of the bunk. "You want to give me fifty bucks?" he asks. "That's something we got to talk about, Lizard."

She turns off the light.

"But Lizard!"

"I'm trying to sleep, George," Lizard says. "You mind?"

Chapter Eleven

THE NEXT MORNING four more desks in Miss Lemon's class are empty. Mick Brady, Lauren Kitts, Jerome Polsky, Nancy Hyppa. That's in addition to Fudge's. As George takes his seat he doesn't say anything. He notices the other kids checking out the empty desks, but they don't say anything either. George hasn't seen so many people not saying anything all at once since his mother died.

Rennie Whitfield is over in the corner talking with the guys who were at the party yesterday. He waves for George to join them, but George shrugs it off with a smile. He never told Rennie he was leaving town and doesn't feel like it now. Too hard. Even if they're not real friends, they could be if he were staying.

Just as the bell is about to ring, Miss Lemon carries a canvas bag into the classroom. "It's time we did art," she says.

George looks up. Once upon a time, they had a real art teacher at Bob Hope Middle. Last fall when the town voted down the school bond issue, they fired Mr. Keller. Now Miss Lemon has to do the art in addition to the regular stuff.

"Anyone know what a shadow box is?" Miss Lemon asks.

"It's like a painting," Marie Kelly says.

"They're in frames like paintings," she says. "But they're three-dimensional. You put real things into them."

She holds up a shadow box for the class to see. It's rectangular. The frame is two feet wide, maybe eighteen inches high. But the back is recessed about six inches. It's a garden scene. George sees the picket fence. The flowers growing over it. A scarecrow.

"The scarecrow is an old doll I found," Miss Lemon tells the class. "The picket fence is Popsicle sticks. The flowers are plastic ones. I found everything I needed in my basement."

"What's this got to do with us?" Miles Chen asks.

"It's the spring art project. You're all going to be making your own shadow box."

"Are we going to make it out of your junk, Miss Lemon?" Weesie Knapp asks.

"No, your junk."

"My family doesn't have a basement," Erik Biondi protests.

"You could find things over at the town dump on Route Three," Misty Snyder tells him.

"Recycling center," Lizard says.

"How's that again?"

"There's no dump on Route Three, Misty."

"Looks like one," Erik Biondi giggles.

"Well, it's not," Lizard says more forcefully. "It's a recycling center. Everything there gets recycled into something else. The tires and the glass, it all gets recycled. Even the garbage. They're making an island of it somewhere in the Pacific."

"Gee, why don't they recycle *you*, Lizard," someone yells.

It isn't funny, but everyone laughs anyway. George cringes. It's not like this is the first time he has ever been embarrassed for Lizard. Doesn't she care that kids make fun of her for collecting empties all over town? Does she have to make it worse by giving lectures about recycling?

Miss Lemon smiles. "Well, if you're looking for materials, why not check out the recycling center?" she suggests. "You're going to have a ball turning what you find there into art."

George hears the groans, from boys mostly. George

wonders if he's the only boy in the class who doesn't complain about the art assignments.

"Oh, come on, boys," Miss Lemon chides. "Give it a shot."

Fern Dachroeden, three rows over, raises her hand. As usual, she doesn't wait for Miss Lemon to call on her before she speaks. "You know what the trouble is? Boys just aren't as good at art as girls!"

"Tell that to Michelangelo," Miss Lemon says. "Or Picasso."

"I meant the boys here in town," Fern explains. She scrounges around in her book bag. "If you don't believe me, take a look at this!"

She waves a notepad in the air. It's George's doodle pad, but it takes him a moment to realize that. Before he can protest, Fern is out of her seat, running down the aisle to hand it to Miss Lemon. "It's George Honiker's," she exclaims. "Look! It's all ugly things like cars, motorbikes, the pumps down at the gas station."

"She stole the doodle pad from George on the bus," Rennie Whitfield shouts.

Miss Lemon doesn't seem to hear Rennie. She's flipping through the pages, studying the drawings.

"It's just doodles," George explains.

Miss Lemon looks up at him. She walks down the aisle and hands the doodle pad to him. "You did these?"

"I know they're ugly," George says. "I don't need anyone to tell me that."

"You draw plain things," she says gently, "but you draw them beautifully. Remember, art doesn't have to be pretty."

George feels his face getting red. It's hard not to be embarrassed.

"I hope you'll do something wonderful for your shadow box, George."

George shrugs. "I can't," he explains. "I got to move out of town with my sister."

"When?" Miss Lemon asks.

"This afternoon," he says. "Right after school."

"The mill?" Miss Lemon asks, but the way she says it, it's clear she knows the answer already.

"Karl," George says, "he's my sister's husband. He had to get a new job right away."

"We're going to miss you, George," she says.

George nods numbly. He keeps his eyes directly on Miss Lemon as she heads back to her desk and picks up some old ribbons there. He's afraid everyone's going to be staring at him, feeling sorry. Slowly he shifts uneasily in his seat.

No one's looking. Everyone's pretending to be busy. Lizard is reading a note Weesie Knapp just handed her. George feels it's like he's already gone.

When school is over for the day, he leaves everything behind, not just the school stuff, but his own stuff too. The wool ski cap that's been in his desk all winter, two issues of *Motor Trends*, the pocket computer game.

All he takes is the doodle pad.

The walls inside the bus station are old yellow tiles. The cement floor is painted dark green. The long benches with the rounded seats and backs are old. George can see dates—1962, 1976, 1959—carved into the dark wood. There's half a dozen green plastic chairs, too, scattered around the station like someone left them there because they were too ugly to take home.

Tucked in a corner are two duffel bags filled with his stuff. His bike leans against the tile wall. The bus company said he can stick his bike in the compartment under the bus.

Mrs. Artoonian drove him, his bags, and his bike down in her pickup after school. Lizard wanted to wait with him till the bus left, but the bus wasn't due for forty minutes, and George wouldn't let her. Good-byes are hard enough without dragging them out. He changed his mind about the rest of the junk he left in his desk. He wants it after all. Lizard promised to send it.

George takes out his doodle pad and looks around for something to draw. There's the newspaper stand, an ATM, a vending machine. He starts drawing the vending machine. He's barely sketched in the outline of the machine when a man with a mustache and his hair in a red-and-white bandanna plunks a suitcase down in front of the machine.

The man starts shaking the machine with both hands. George jumps to his feet. He doesn't know if the guy is a thief or maybe just a nut, but someone should call a cop. He looks around. An old woman is snoring on a bench. Two young men are yakking away in some foreign language behind him. No cops. No one who seems about to go for one either.

When George turns back, the man has got the vending machine open.

"Hey!" George shouts. "You're not supposed to—"

"Hey, buddy," the man says, "I work for the company."

"Huh?"

The man opens the suitcase. Inside it's all candy bars and little bags of potato chips.

George scratches his head. Not that he ever thought the machines just filled themselves, but he never imagined it was someone's job.

"You want a Snickers?"

"Free, you mean?"

George takes the candy bar and sticks it in the chest pocket of his shirt. "Saving it for later," he tells the man.

"How about another for now?"

"Okay," George says.

This one he unwraps. It's a Mounds. Once, the coconut made him throw up, but how's he going to explain that to the man? He sits down, takes a cautious bite, puts the rest of the candy bar beside him on the bench.

He starts doodling. If he's drawing, maybe the man won't notice he's not eating. He decides to draw the inside of the vending machine, minus the man. George doesn't do people yet.

It only takes another minute or two for the man to refill the machine. "Mounds is my oldest kid's favorite candy bar," he says.

"How many kids you got?" George asks.

"I got four."

"You make enough money filling candy machines to have four kids?"

The man shrugs. "Yeah, but they don't get to eat anything but candy and chips."

"You mean it?"

The man chuckles. "Don't worry," he says. "The company's got a terrific dental plan."

George waits until the man is gone before he pulls

his wallet from his back pocket. Five tens. They're all there, looking so stiff and new George is inclined to think Lizard washes and irons her money.

The lamp above the ticket window is on. All George has to do is buy his ticket. The next bus for Pittsfield leaves in twenty minutes. All he has to do is buy his ticket and he'll be on his way.

There's a pay phone by the door. George heads for it. He dials. When the operator asks, he tells her, "It's collect from George." He listens to the phone ringing, doesn't expect anyone to answer, can't help feeling startled when someone picks up.

"Dad?"

"George? Hey, buddy, what's up?"

He just blurts it out. "You didn't send the money like you said."

"I'll get to it, I promise," his father says. "Don't you worry."

"Tammy says you haven't sent money since last fall."

Silence at the other end. "You didn't need to know about that, George. She shouldn't have told you. Karl said you guys could manage."

"The mill closed," George announces.

"Oh, no, what's Karl going to do?"

"He already did it."

"Huh?"

"They moved yesterday so he could get another job.

I got to go today. They couldn't even wait till school was over."

"Tammy and Karl have to think about that baby, I guess."

"Come home, Dad," George says. "Please."

"You're better off with Tammy and Karl right now."

"I want to be with you, Dad."

"There's no way I can make a living in East Siena," his father tells him. "You know that already, George. There's not even the mill now. What the heck would I do there?"

"You could fill candy machines," George says.

"Where the heck do you get these ideas from, George?"

"They got great benefits, Dad."

Another silence at the other end. Then George hears his father chuckling again. "Filling candy machines? You think that's going to get us that nice house I promised you, George?"

"But we'd be together," George mumbles.

"Just hang in there a little longer, George. I got some new plans. This time they'll pan out, I promise you."

"What happened to the ostriches?"

"You ever eat ostrich, George?" his father asks. "Tastes like rubber."

"Did you get fired, Dad?"

"I was going to quit anyway, George. I heard there's

this big oil field up in Canada. Everyone says the money's going to be in oil. You still want that big swimming pool, don't you, George?"

"I guess so."

"Then go to Tammy," his father says. "It won't be much longer. I promise, George."

George nods, but he doesn't say anything.

"You still there, George? You didn't go hanging up on me or anything, did you?"

"It's okay, Dad," George sighs.

"That's my boy," his father says. "That's my George."

George nods again. Hangs up. When he turns, he sees the duffel bags and the bike in the corner. He counts the change in his pocket. He's got enough quarters for two lockers. Won't have to break one of Lizard's tens. It's a sign, he decides.

When the duffels are safely in the lockers, he grabs hold of the bike and wheels it through the bus station. Just as he comes outside he sees the Pittsfield bus pulling into the station.

That's not a sign.

(After a while you know how to call them.)

No way is he catching that bus, or the one that leaves in three hours. Can't go back to Lizard's. He knows that for sure. Mrs. Artoonian would put him up one more night, then ship him out on the bus the next morning. He's not taking that bus either.

Once he has walked the bike onto the street, he gets on. There's traffic. Lots of it. Trucks mostly, headed for the interstate. He coughs as he inhales a blast of carbon monoxide.

He gets on the bike, starts to weave between two semis waiting for the light to change. He knows where he's going. It's just something that came to him. If he thinks about it, he'll get scared.

So he doesn't think about it.

Chapter Twelve

GEORGE IS WIDE awake. He is lying on a small wicker sofa. The night air is cool. Lucky for him there was a small blanket draped over the back of a chair. It's pulled up to George's eyes. They are wide open, peering around the room, seeing shadows turn into eerie shapes that could be anything. He listens to the river rushing below the boathouse.

He's never been so tired in his whole life. But he's too scared to sleep. Do they have night watchmen here? Do they have dogs maybe? He hears a floorboard creak. He holds his breath. Another floorboard creaks. Someone's coming up the stairs. The footsteps are coming closer. They're crossing the room. He sees the beam from a flashlight flying all around the wall. The footsteps are practically on top of him now. He closes his eyes. What's he thinking? That they don't arrest intruders if they pretend to be asleep?

"George?"

Even with his eyelids closed, he can feel the flashlight on his face.

"I know you're awake."

He relaxes, but only slightly. He knows it's Brett, but it could still mean trouble.

"How do you know?" he challenges.

"No one sleeps with their eyelids clenched," she says.

Reluctantly he opens his eyes. As the blanket falls to the floor he sits up. Brett's turned on a lamp now. She's as pretty as he remembers. Still wearing the big boots, but she's got on a white sweater that looks as soft and fluffy as the lamb it came from.

"You said you had plenty of room," he mumbles by way of explanation.

"I assumed you'd give us some warning," she points out.

"I can leave in the morning," he says. "I can leave now. You don't have to call the cops if you want me to go." He jumps up from the sofa. She gently pushes him back.

"You're not leaving at all," Brett says, sitting down next to him. "I'll square it with Ga."

He exhales the breath that he's been holding since he heard her footsteps. "You don't have to, you know."

"I want to, George. Honest. It's my fault and I want to help."

"But—"

"Breakfast's at seven thirty," she tells him. "Don't be late. Ga is a stickler for punctuality."

She turns the lamp off. Guiding herself with the flashlight, she walks across the floor and down the stairs. In a moment he hears her latching the door.

George lies back down on the sofa. He pulls the blanket up to his chin, snuggles his head into the pillow. Listening to the river, he falls asleep.

Chapter Thirteen

WHEN GEORGE WAKES up, it's almost eight. The clothes he is wearing are the only clothes he brought, so he's already dressed. He didn't bring a toothbrush, so there's no reason to bother with that. As soon as he slips on his sneakers he tears down the stairs and out of the boathouse. When he arrives at the main house, he's panting so hard that he has to catch his breath before stepping into the dining room.

The three of them are already eating their breakfast. Mrs. Whitfield sits at the head of the mahogany table. George is surprised to see anyone so dressed up for breakfast. She's wearing a pink suit and a pearl necklace.

Brett and Rennie sit on opposite sides, facing each other. There are nine other chairs, but only the place next to Brett is set with silver and a cloth napkin.

"For me?" he asks.

"For you, George. For you since seven thirty, in fact," Mrs. Whitfield says, looking up from her coffee and checking her wristwatch. "Punctuality is a sign of a gentleman, young man. If Rennie and Brett's parents weren't out of town just now, they'd be here at seven thirty too. There's food on the sideboard in case you'd like more than just the pleasure of our company."

On the sideboard are silver dishes filled with scrambled eggs, bacon and sausages, two kinds of muffins, toast, pancakes, even corn flakes. On a tray are three different pitchers of juice—tomato, orange, something brown that could be prune. A compote of mixed fruit fills a silver bowl. George has never seen anything like this in someone's home.

"Hey, it's just like the cafeteria at school," George exclaims.

He pours himself some orange juice and fills a bowl with corn flakes. It's not until he's plunked himself and his food down next to Brett that he remembers it's the same breakfast he has every day.

He sips his juice. At home he chugs. It drives Tammy crazy. If Tammy got herself a dining table as long as a football field and a chandelier that weighs a thousand pounds, he'd sip in the trailer, too.

"You really going to stay here?" Rennie asks, smiling slightly.

"For a little while, I guess," George says as he takes a sip of his juice. "If you let me."

"It's so cool," Rennie says admiringly. "I never would have had the nerve."

"Well, it's our fault, really," Brett announces. "We did everything we could to close down the mill. It's only right we take him in, at least for a while."

"Brett, he is not one of your causes," Mrs. Whitfield says as she carefully spreads butter onto a tiny wedge of crustless toast.

A maid in a uniform with a little white cap enters, carrying a silver coffeepot. She pours coffee into Mrs. Whitfield's cup. Mrs. Whitfield nods slightly, imperceptibly. As the maid leaves, Mrs. Whitfield turns her gaze from her cup to George.

"I like you, George, and you may stay here with us as long as you don't spray-paint horrid words on the tennis court!"

George is bewildered. "Why would I do something like that?"

"Oh, Ga," Brett says, shaking her head. "Shame on you!"

"We had to have the whole court resurfaced after last summer's visit by those dreadful children," Mrs. Whitfield protests. "Cost a fortune, too. You'll never find me giving one more dime to the Fresh Air Fund."

"George isn't like that!"

Mrs. Whitfield shakes her head disdainfully. "Boys are boys. I bet you know plenty of foul words, don't you?"

"A couple maybe," George admits.

Mrs. Whitfield harrumphs. "You're twelve years old, aren't you? The same age as Rennie."

"Last winter."

"Then you know plenty," Mrs. Whitfield announces. "I wasn't born yesterday. How's your spelling, George?"

"Oh, I'm a good speller, Mrs. Whitfield," he assures her.

"Well, that's a relief, I must say," Mrs. Whitfield says. "If you're going to defile my property with vulgar words, the least you can do is spell them correctly. You'll be in the blue room, George."

"He's bunking in with me," Rennie says.

"If you prefer," Mrs. Whitfield says.

"You sure?" George asks Rennie.

"There's two beds," Rennie assures him. "There's plenty of room."

"Whatever," Mrs. Whitfield says. "It won't do for the boy to camp out in the boathouse one more night. Jenkins will fetch your things while you're at school, George."

"Things?" George asks. "What things?"

"Well, clothes and toothbrushes," Mrs. Whitfield says.

"I left them at the bus station," George tells her. "In two lockers."

"At the bus station?" Mrs. Whitfield asks. "What were you doing at the bus station?"

Brett breaks in. "Ga, I told you."

"Oh, yes, making your getaway! Do you have the keys, George?"

"Yes."

"Give them here, then," Mrs. Whitfield says.

It's a command. It doesn't occur to George to ask what she wants them for. He just automatically pulls the keys from his pocket, hands them to Brett, who hands them on to her grandmother.

"When Murdoch drives me into town this morning, we'll stop by the bus station," the old woman declares.

"But they're my things," George protests. "I can get them."

"You should be on your way to school," Mrs. Whitfield says. "Both of you."

"Come on, George," Rennie says. "Or we'll miss the school bus."

Rennie is already pushing back his chair. George stands up, follows Rennie into the hall. Rennie grabs his book bag. George remembers he left his books behind at school the day before.

Rennie holds the front door for George, follows him outside. The boys walk down the white gravel drive.

"When you invited me to your birthday party, you

probably figured I'd go home afterward. You don't have to put me up if you don't feel like it. I got other places I could stay." It's not true, but he's got to give Rennie an out, doesn't he?

Rennie puts his hand on George's shoulder. "Most of the guys," he says, "they like to come here, but they never ask me back to their house."

"Me either," George points out. "I never asked you back to mine."

"But you would now, I bet," Rennie says. "Now that we're friends, I mean. It's just that now you don't have a house to invite me back to. That's all."

"Oh, sure," George assures him. "It's not your fault your folks are loaded, is it?"

Rennie grins. "I should tell my folks that," he says.

"Where do you keep them?" George asks. "Your folks, I mean."

"They're away right now," Rennie tells him. "They'll be back."

George sees the bus coming to a stop at the end of the Whitfields' driveway. Rennie breaks into a run. George runs after him.

"Sorry, Mr. Tiani," Rennie gasps as he gets on the bus.

"Next time I'm not waiting," Mr. Tiani says.

When George gets on, he sees Mr. Tiani's eyebrows go up about two inches.

"Moving up in the world, huh, George?"

George frowns, even though he's got to expect it. He sees Lizard sitting with some of the other kids from the trailer park toward the back of the bus. She sees George. Her jaw drops and her eyes bulge out a little more than usual. He waves, but he doesn't go to the back of the bus.

He sits next to Rennie instead.

Chapter Fourteen

RENNIE JOINS THE Frisbee game in the parking lot. Most of the girls cluster around Sallie Gardenia, squealing over her latest E-mail from some boy. Some of the boys shake George's hand. Whether it's for staying in East Siena or for crashing at the Whitfields', George isn't sure.

George walks into Bob Hope Middle by himself.

His feet clatter on the hard linoleum. The noise echoes against the tile walls. He sees desks stacked outside the classrooms. Outside Miss Lemon's classroom there are six of them. One for each kid who has left school on account of the mill closing down.

Make that five kids. One of them missed the bus yesterday.

George wants his pocket computer game back.

He'd like his blue ski cap and the two copies of *Motor Trends*. He starts going through the desks one by one. He finds Fudge Sudow's baseball cards in one desk. He finds Nancy Hyppa's plastic barrettes in another.

George's desk is the last one. He recognizes the crack that's the shape of Lake Erie in the Formica. When he looks inside, it's empty. Except for the textbooks, of course. But that's not what he is looking for.

"George?"

Lizard's wearing pink plastic bracelets. There's got to be half a dozen on each arm. "I picked up your stuff yesterday," she tells him. "Like you asked."

"I'll come by for it," he says, "when I get a chance."

"You could have stayed with us, you know," Lizard tells him. "It's not like we don't have enough space. You didn't have to go stay with *them*."

How is he supposed to explain this one to her? George scratches the side of his head. Doesn't she realize a top bunk in a crowded trailer hardly qualifies as "enough" anything?

The bell rings. Lizard turns, heads into Miss Lemon's class. Just as she's about to open the classroom door he catches up with her.

"I got your money," he says.

"On you?"

"Back at the Whitfields'," he says. "I'll remember tomorow."

"It was a gift," she says.

"But I didn't need it," he says. "Don't you want it back?"

But she's already run into the classroom.

Chapter Fifteen

RENNIE'S ROOM, IT turns out, is slightly larger than Karl and Tammy's entire trailer. It's on the second floor, at the front of the house. French doors open onto a balcony. It would be perfect, George decides, for visiting royalty. On state occasions they could wave to the crowd in the driveway below.

At the far end of the room it's like someone went on a tear at Circuit City. A laptop, two televisions, a DVD player, of course. Shelves are stacked with video games, a Game Boy, DVDs and CDs. Dozens of photographs—big, small, in between—are in silver frames. Rennie's in almost all of them. Rennie on skis, waving at the camera. Rennie waving at the camera from a sailboat, Rennie waving at the camera from the Eiffel Tower, Rennie waving as he rides a dolphin.

There's plenty of space left over for books. Rennie,

however, has only three. A hardcover *Robinson Crusoe*, the spine of which is so stiff that George has to be the first person ever to open it. A paperback *Encyclopedia of Baseball* that is so worn out that pages fall to the floor when George looks at it. A yearbook from Allcroft School in New Hampshire. CLASS OF 1974 is embossed on the cover. George has never seen so many teenage boys with such good complexions. Either someone retouched the photos or rich kids don't get zits.

"That's my dad's prep school," Rennie says.

George nods, puts the book back on the shelf. "You going there?"

"In ninth grade probably," Rennie says.

The rest of Rennie's bedroom is mostly a train setup. It's perched on what looks like a billiard table. The train must have fifteen cars to it, and the tracks go through a farm with a barn and sheep in the field, and then a town with a village square and a big white church, and then along the seashore before they go through a city with incredibly authentic skyscrapers.

George hasn't ever seen a train set like this one. Not in a store. Not even in the movies. He's looking around for some place to turn it on, when he spots his duffel bags. They are on one of the four-poster beds. Even before he gets to the bed, though, he sees they are completely empty.

"What the—?"

"Looking for something?"

"My stuff," George mutters.

"Check the closet?"

"Huh?"

"Jenkins probably unpacked for you," Rennie suggests.

"Jenkins?"

"The butler," Rennie reminds him.

"He'd do that?"

"That's what servants do."

George opens the closet. It's enormous. There's even a light that goes on automatically. On one side there's a blue blazer hanging, a half a dozen pairs of pants—gray flannel, chinos, khakis—some shirts. On the other side are shelves—more shirts, some jeans folded up, half a dozen sweaters. And shoes, too. Sneakers, deck shoes, Loafers, dress-up tie shoes, even a pair of riding boots. Not on the floor, either. In the shelves. They're so shiny they look like Rennie never wore any of them before.

"You sure got a lot of clothes," George says.

"Oh, my closet's over there," Rennie says, pointing to a door on the other side of the room. "That's your stuff in the closet."

"It's not! I never saw these clothes before."

"Ga went shopping."

"For me?" George gasps incredulously.

"What's the matter?" Rennie says, laughing a bit. "Don't you like Ga's taste?"

George gives the clothes another look-over. It's not just a lot of clothes, more clothes than he's ever had. But they're really nice clothes too. Expensive, he means. Even George can tell these aren't from the sale racks at Kmart.

"Are you kidding?" he asks. "They must have cost a bundle."

Still shaking his head in amazement, he walks out of the closet. He checks out the duffel bags again. "You know what happened to the rest of my stuff?"

Rennie shrugs. "Ga probably told Jenkins to chuck it."

"She'd throw my clothes away?"

"Hey, you don't really *want* to dress like the kids down at the trailer park, do you?" he says.

"There's nothing wrong with those kids," George protests.

"I'm talking about the clothes, George."

"What about my other stuff?" George asks. "Pictures. Family stuff. About my dad, mostly. From the businesses he had. It was all in this big manila envelope."

"It's around somewhere," Rennie says. "It'll turn up. No one's going to throw away anything unless it's garbage."

"You think?" George asks worriedly.

"I know!" Rennie grins.

Rennie's got a dentist appointment in town. The boys start into the hall. At the top of the stairs Rennie puts an arm around George's shoulder. "I'm glad you're here, George," he says.

Nodding slightly, George pauses. He's about to say how glad he is too, but Rennie has already run down the stairs ahead of him.

George hears a loud, sharp clicking on the marble floor below. Mrs. Whitefield. Her heels seem even higher than usual. She's looking especially businesslike this afternoon in a gray suit, with two strands of pearls around her neck. She's carrying a purse. Her hair looks almost silver. It looks starched, George decides.

"Wait for me in the car, Rennie," she commands her grandson. "I need a word with George."

"Did I do something wrong?" George asks nervously.

"Not yet, dear," Mrs. Whitfield says. Her glance, however, lingers on Rennie. She waits until he's closed the front door before she turns back to George.

"The clothes, George," she says. "I hope you don't mind."

"Mind?"

"Rennie and Brett have fits when I buy them clothes. You're not going to be so awful about it, are you?"

"No, I don't mind," George says.

"I knew you'd be a sport about it."

"It's just, I don't know what happened to my—"

"If you don't like something, it's all right," she goes on. "Just pretend you do. I don't know where everyone got the impression it's so important to be honest about everything!"

"But I really like—"

Mrs. Whitfield tilts her head, studying his face. "You need a decent haircut, George. I'll make an appointment for you."

"An appointment? My sister cuts my hair."

"Your sister is in Pittsfield. That's a bit far for a haircut, isn't it?"

"How much is a haircut going to cost?"

"Just put it on my account," she says as she walks across the hall to the front door.

"It's one thing to let me stay here, but I can't take—"

"The door, George. Please."

"But I need to tell you, Mrs. Whitfield. You can't spend money on someone you don't know."

"George? The door?"

George opens the front door for her. The Mercedes is idling just outside, Murdoch at the wheel. Rennie is sitting in the backseat.

"But Mrs. Whitfield!" he exclaims as he follows her onto the front steps.

She nods toward the Mercedes. George gets it finally. Mrs. Whitfield doesn't open doors. Ever. He starts to open the front door on the passenger side for her. She shakes her head. "I don't think Murdoch would approve, George," she whispers.

George opens the rear door.

"I enjoyed our little talk very much, George," she says as she slips in next to Rennie. "You're a nice boy. Not at all like those other children from the Fresh Air Fund."

"But I'm not from the Fresh Air Fund!" George protests.

"The door, George. Please."

"Sorry, Mrs. Whitfield," George says, shutting it.

Murdoch puts the engine in gear. The tires spit white gravel on George's shoes as the Mercedes picks up speed.

George checks out his closet again. The clothes. He still can't believe it. Slowly he takes the blazer from the hanger, tries it on. He steps into the bathroom to check himself in the mirror there. Well, maybe he could use a haircut after all.

Something catches his eye. It's in the wastebasket next to the sink. It's blue. Familiar. George takes a step toward it. It's the shirt his dad gave him for Christmas. It's his favorite shirt. It's almost new, too. Not like his other clothes. How'd someone get the nerve to throw it out? he wonders.

As he grabs the shirt he sees the familiar manila envelope at the bottom of the wastebasket. He reaches for it. A plastic roller skating key slips out, clattering onto the tile floor. LORD OF THE RINK. It's embossed on the handle. George smiles. It's the giveaway his dad designed for the roller-skating rink.

George sits on the edge of the bathtub. He takes out a stack of old snapshots held together with a rubber band. There's his dad with that little fish he caught. An old one with George on a rocking horse and Tammy standing in front of the Christmas tree they had at the old house. And there's one of his mom. George looks at that one for a long time, then puts the pictures back in the envelope.

He walks back to the bedroom. The closet door is still open. He hides the envelope under the stack of sweaters. He puts the plastic skate key in his pocket.

Chapter Sixteen

EVERY TIME GEORGE approaches Lizard at school, she turns away. It makes him all the more determined to return the money to her. But how? He can't mail it, can he?

After school he rides his bike from the Whitfields' down to the trailer park. It's late afternoon. The sun's in his eyes all the way to the Versailles.

"Lizard!" he shouts, jumping off the bike and letting it coast into the bushes.

"They're not home, George."

It's Mr. Kretch, sitting on the grass, drinking a soda. Like always, he's cold and wearing a gray sweater all buttoned up over one of his favorite Hawaiian shirts. He's retired now but says he's planning on staying at the Versailles till his daughter puts him in a rest home.

"You know when they'll be back, Mr. Kretch?" George asks.

Mr. Kretch takes a last swig of the soda, sets the can on the grass. "Since when does anyone ever tell me anything?" he asks.

George shrugs. He takes his doodle pad from his back pocket, the pencil from the pocket on the front of his shirt.

Lizard,
Thanks for the fifty.
Sorry I got you so mad.
I didn't mean to.
—*George*

He folds the paper, sticks the five ten-dollar bills in the crease. Then he writes Lizard's name on the outside. For a moment he considers leaving it with Mr. Kretch. Thinks again. Mr. Kretch might read the note. He might even steal the money.

"Can I have the rest of your soda, Mr. Kretch?"

"There is no rest of it," he laughs.

"Just the can."

"What the heck do I need an empty can of soda for?"

George rolls the note with the bills inside up tight. It's as narrow as a cigarette. He sticks the roll into the hole at the top of the can and drops the can on the grass. She may not find it till tomorrow, but she'll find it all right, he figures.

"So long, Mr. Kretch," George says as he gets back on his bike.

"Where the heck are you going, George?" he asks. "Didn't your sister move out of town or something?"

"Or something," he calls over his shoulder as he pedals through the Versailles Trailer Park gates and onto the highway.

Chapter Seventeen

"I TALKED TO George's sister last night," Mrs. Whitfield announces at breakfast.

"You called Tammy?" George asks. Suddenly, he's fearful.

"Tammy? Yes. What a name. So peculiar. No, I didn't call her. She called here, as a matter of fact. Quite late last night. Apparently, she called the lady who runs the trailer park—"

"Mrs. Artoonian?"

"Yes, another peculiar name, if you ask me," she says, with a dismissive wave of the hand. "Apparently, she did a rather poor job explaining your current situation, or your sister wouldn't have been so upset when I spoke to her."

"Is she mad?" George asks. "Does she want me to come up to Pittsfield?"

"I explained that was out of the question," Mrs. Whitfield says. "I did what I could to assure the poor woman that we weren't holding you here against your will. Or starving you. She said she'd like to hear it from you. But it was much too late. I explained you had gone to bed hours before."

"Did she leave a number?"

"They're not getting a phone right away. Imagine. No phone!" old Mrs. Whitfield says.

"Will she call back?" George asks.

"Oh, probably," Mrs. Whitfield says. "But you've got to tell her I'm being nice to you, George, or she might throw me in jail. I don't think jail would be any fun for me at all. What do you think, George?"

"I think you'd better watch your step, Mrs. Whitfield," George says.

Everyone laughs at that. Rennie. Brett. Mrs. Whitfield most of all.

Fern Dachroeden's doing a shadow box like a little theater because she's going to be an actress when she grows up. Erik Biondi's using his Cleveland Indians memorabilia for his. Norman Kremitz is doing paper dolls, and he doesn't seem to care that everyone, even the girls, is laughing about it.

"Look around your own home," Miss Lemon suggests. "Where you live says a lot about you."

George smiles at that one. The Whitfields' house says nothing about him. That's the best part of staying there, he thinks.

George sees a batch of color snapshots on the table by the door. Elephants. Tigers. Rhinos. Even zebras. African tribespeople in colorful robes dancing in a circle.

"Dad took the photos," Brett explains. "He's on safari, but he sent them last week." As usual, she is dressed for riding in her shining boots, carrying a brown velvet hat that looks just like a helmet.

"In Africa?" George exclaims. Even as he says it he's embarrassed. He knows they don't have safaris anywhere else but Africa. "How long has he been gone?"

"A month maybe."

"You're not sure?"

"Dad takes an awful lot of trips," Brett explains. "It's hard to keep track. Come with me. I'll show you the stables."

"You got a horse, too?" he exclaims.

"Several, in fact," Brett says. "Do you ride?"

George shakes his head.

"Want to learn?"

"I've got the clothes for it now, I guess."

"If you'd rather not—"

"No, I'd like to," George says. "If I don't have to wear the clothes."

"The jeans you've got on will do fine," Brett assures him as she leads him out the front door and down the driveway. The stables are on the other side of the orchard. The last of the blossoms have fallen. George can see them in the grass now. But there must have been thousands of them. Millions, more likely. What happened? Did they just disappear?

"Does your dad travel for his work?" George asks.

"Oh, travel is Dad's great passion," Brett tells him.

"But what's your dad do?" George asks.

"Oh, lots of things. Not just travel. He's very good at golf. He does a lot of collecting. He's got some charities he's very involved with too."

"I meant for a living," George says. "What's your dad do for a living?"

Brett smiles. "Oh, he had a job once, but it was long before Rennie or I was born. I don't think he liked it very much."

"So he just quit?"

"Well, something like that," Brett says, shrugging.

George still isn't sure he believes it. He never heard of a man not working, unless he was sick or crazy, and he's not about to get into that stuff with Brett.

Through the trees George sees the stables ahead. They are stone. Same green paint on the doors as up at the main house. Same white trim. The doors are big and cut in half so the horses can look out. George guesses it must be boring to be a horse, even a rich one.

Brett points to a horse grazing in the corral. "That's Amber," she tells George. "She's Mother's prize hunter, sixteen hands high. The others are with Mother at a horse show in Maryland this week. Amber had to stay home. She threw a shoe and hurt her leg."

"She didn't go on the safari with your dad?"

"Who? Amber?"

"No, I mean your mom, of course. Did she go on safari?"

"Oh, never!" Brett laughs "Mother likes only the animals she can ride. They're her whole life, really. She even sleeps with them."

"Can't horses be left alone at night?"

"They're high-strung, especially when they're away from home."

"She could hire someone, couldn't she?" George asks.

"The horses are practically family, George! Mother would never leave them with strangers."

"If there really is reincarnation," George tells her, "next time I'm coming back as one of your family's horses."

Chapter Eighteen

IT'S AFTER SCHOOL the next day. The bus has just dropped Rennie and George off. The boys are walking along the driveway back to the Whitfields' house.

"What are you putting in your shadow box?" George asks.

"Not sure yet," Rennie replies. "I need an idea. You got any for me, George?"

"You could do your motorboat."

"How?"

"Paint the shore for your background. Use some bubble wrap for the water. You could have the front half of a model boat coming out of it."

Rennie likes the idea. "It would be kind of neat," he says. "No one else would do that! You know what you're going to do for your shadow box, George?"

"I was thinking I could do an engine," George tells him.

"You're kidding!" Rennie exclaims. Clearly, he's impressed. "How would you pull that off in three dimensions?"

"I could make a hood," George tells him. "I could put it on a little hinge so that when you open it, you see the whole thing. The manifold. The flywheel. The gaskets. I could even do a radiator, I bet."

"Where are you going to find the stuff to make it from?"

"Murdoch's got to have some scrap metal in the garage," George says. "I bet Jenkins has a saw that cuts metal. I got it all planned out."

"That would be the coolest shadow box of all," Rennie assures him.

George nods happily. "I know."

Chapter Nineteen

WHEN GEORGE CHECKED the garage for scrap, Murdoch told him they didn't keep their scraps. "We put them in the trash, where they belong," he explained. Rennie says Murdoch's a worse snob than Ga. He's probably right, too, George thinks. But at least Murdoch offered to drive George down to the recycling center, so he's not all bad, is he?

George sits alone in the back of the Mercedes as Murdoch drives along Route 3. There's plenty of traffic, both directions, so the air is foul. George pushes the button on the door and the window rolls up. Here and there is a regular house, but mostly it's strip malls. Dunkin' Donuts. Car washes. Dry cleaners. It's ugly. No two ways about it. Who wouldn't prefer to live anywhere else if they could?

The chain-link fence outside the recycling center is

beginning to rust. The dirt road is badly rutted, and the cars and trucks crawl in. "Would you mind walking, George?" Murdoch asks. "The car just wasn't built for that kind of road. I'll wait for you here."

George walks along the shoulder. The weeds are up to his knees. It's a recycling station. What can you expect? It's like an open-air market. Except no one's selling anything. Apart from the cans, you can't get any money for your junk either. The back of one old, derelict moving van is used for newspapers. They're stacked almost twenty feet high, too. There's a place for cans that you can't redeem. There's another place for glass.

As George comes to the end of the road he finds old furniture. Couches, chairs, tables. On the far side, he finds the stuff he's been looking for. Mostly it's what people couldn't even unload at their yard sales. Books. Records. Toys.

Pots and pans. A vacuum cleaner. Half a dozen Sears lawn mowers. One of the mowers is falling apart, George notices.

It takes a while to extract the parts he wants. By the time he's through, he's got more than enough for the shadow box. Once it's crammed into his book bag, he starts back down the dirt road to Route 3. A car is parked at the side of the road. It's a wreck, with psychedelic painting covering every inch. The tires are painted. Who wouldn't recognize it? Even if Mrs. Artoonian weren't loading tires into the back of it, he'd know her car anywhere.

"Well, for Pete's sake," she exclaims. "I never expected to see you again, George. Certainly not here at the dump."

"Recycling center," he reminds her.

"Whatever," Mrs. Artoonian says as she lights up. "Lizard tells me you moved in with the Whitfields in that big house of theirs. Look at you! I never saw you wearing clothes like that before! You look like you belong up there in the Heights, a real ritzy kid."

"I'm still me, Mrs. Artoonian."

"What you got in there, George?" she asks.

"Things," he explains. "For school."

"Well, you can't go wrong at the dump, can you? The price is right," she says, laughing and coughing.

"It's not a dump. It's a recycling—"

"Yeah, sure," Mrs. Artoonian says agreeably. "I'm getting tires today. You want to give a hand?"

"You can't use them as spares," he tells her. "They're not safe."

"Planters, George."

"Huh?"

"I'm going to circle my fountain with them and fill the holes with soil and put flowers in them," she says.

"Real flowers?" he asks.

"What do I need real flowers for?"

"Well, you're using real soil, aren't you?"

"You can put plastic flowers in real soil, George," Mrs. Artoonian points out. "It doesn't damage the plastic any."

He sees Lizard in the front seat. He waves at her. She shakes her head. What's that supposed to mean?

"Hey, Lizard, did you get the money?"

"Next time just hand it to me. You don't need to put it in a soda can."

She rolls up the window.

He shrugs. The Mercedes is idling out on Route 3. George walks faster now. He doesn't want to keep Murdoch waiting.

Chapter Twenty

IN ONE HAND Mrs. Whitfield carries a small notebook. In the other, the thinnest gold pen George ever saw in his life. "Now, let's get down to business," she says, adjusting her eyeglasses and opening the little notebook on the coffee table. She uncaps the pen and holds it poised above the paper. "We've got plans to make, George."

"Plans?" George asks uncertainly.

"Lessons," Mrs. Whitfield informs him.

"Like school, you mean?"

"Worse than school," Brett warns him, laughing slightly. "Sure you don't want to make a run for it? Your sister's might not look so bad once you see what Ga's got in mind for you, George."

"Please, Brett," Mrs. Whitfield says, not even cracking a smile. "George might not be so ungrateful as you and Rennie are. He might even appreciate the opportunity to improve himself a bit."

"Don't let her push you around, George," Brett protests, "You're entitled to a little fun while you're here."

"Everything in life isn't supposed to be fun, young lady," Mrs. Whitfield says, sticking one end of the little gold pen in the corner of her mouth. "I've made a list of all the lessons I could arrange for you, George. You just tell me which ones interest you. My, isn't this exciting?"

"How many times do I have to do these lessons?" he asks suspiciously.

"Once a week," Mrs. Whitfield explains. "Or so."

"Any homework?"

"Oh, nothing like that!" she assures him. "We just have someone come to the house, give you the lesson, and then go home, and that's it till next time. So convenient."

"Well, I guess, if there's no homework," George says.

"How would you like to start with French lessons?" Mrs. Whitfield asks, checking her pad. "Such an asset for a young man of the world. So cultured!"

"French?" George asks. "You mean like the language?"

Mrs. Whitfield nods hopefully. "You'd like Madame de la Roche. She's so colorful. Eats snails every day."

"Snails?" George asks. "I'd rather eat nails."

"Oh, George! You are so amusing," Mrs. Whitfield says, laughing like a little bell.

"No snails!"

"Well, I suppose," she says, going back to her list. "How about dancing? That's a must!"

"Dancing?"

"You'd have to wear a suit, of course. I'll take you into town tomorrow for it. We can spend the afternoon shopping!"

"No suit!"

"I had a feeling that wasn't going to fly," Mrs. Whitfield admits. "Well, then, how about tennis?"

"I already play."

"Well?"

"Well enough," George says. "I learned at Y camp last summer."

"Sailing? I bet you don't already sail, do you, George?"

"Where am I supposed to sail after I leave here?"

"Oh, this is hopeless," Mrs. Whitfield announces. "Why don't you tell me what kinds of lessons you want to take?"

"How about woodworking?" George suggests.

"Too dusty, George. You wouldn't like it. You'd be covered in sawdust!"

"How about mechanics?"

"Mechanics?" Mrs. Whitfield asks slowly, cautiously,

as if the word were new to her. "As in, how to fix an automobile?"

"Yeah," George says eagerly. "It would be cool. You think you could get someone up here to teach me engines?"

"Oh, George," Mrs. Whitfield says. "You don't need to learn such things. You're a bright boy. Once you're out of college, you can just hire someone when your auto breaks down!"

"But I want to do it myself," George insists, sinking back into the couch in frustration.

"I've got big plans for you, George. I want you to be a little gentleman"—she scowls—"not some dreadful grease monkey! Engines are a bit common, don't you think?"

"I never thought about it like that," he admits.

"Why not let George do what he wants?" Brett suggests. "It's his life, you know."

"George will come around!" Mrs. Whitfield insists, eyes still intent on the list. "George has a lot of potential. He's intelligent. He's good looking. Don't you see it, Brett? With a little help, he could become the real thing."

He smiles. He could do a lot worse, he thinks. He gets to live with the richest people in town, doesn't he? He shares the same room with the richest kid in town too. Eats the same food. Gets the same clothes.

Even the same haircut. Gets the same lessons if he wants.

So what if he'll never really be the real thing? What he's got now is close enough.

That night, the boys are in their room, working on their shadow boxes. Rennie's looks like something already. He's sawed a toy boat in half and glued the front to the box. He's got the bubble wrap at the bottom, and it almost looks like water, too. He's drawing himself in the background so it looks like he's water-skiing. It's very cool. Very classy.

George's shadow box is scattered like spare parts across the table he uses as a desk. He's not sure he wants to do his engine anymore. If he could think of something else, something that wasn't so common, he would do it instead.

George hears a horn blasting outside. A car skids to a stop on the gravel in the driveway below. Rennie heads for the balcony. It's a red sports car, top down.

"Hey, Dad! Hey, Dad!" he shouts. He turns back to George. "You got to meet my dad, George! Come on downstairs."

"You go," George says, suddenly feeling very uncomfortable. "I'll meet him later. You go ahead."

"Okay," Rennie says, and steps toward the door. "But don't take too long. My dad is really a cool guy."

Chapter Twenty-One

RENNIE'S DAD IS cool, too. He's got a tan like someone in an ad. He's friendly. Asks George lots of questions. Doesn't talk about himself. When he decides to take Rennie to the hunting lodge they own up in Michigan, he makes sure to invite George along too.

George says he can't go.

"I got to work on my shadow box," he explains, even though a minute ago he had decided definitely that he wasn't going to do it.

Well, he's not about to tell Rennie he's jealous, is he?

(George can pretend that Rennie's things are his things too. But even he can't pretend when it comes to fathers.)

Chapter Twenty-Two

NOW THAT HE'S told Rennie he's doing the shadow box, George has got to do it. He works all weekend on it. From the lawn mower cover he's fashioned a hood. He's even made a medallion for it. There are two headlights, too. Glass from two old flashlights. When you pull up the hood, it's like looking into a real engine. Everything's there. The manifold. The battery. The blue fluid to clean the windshield. There's at least half a dozen cables that he cut from an old extension cord he found at the recycling center too. When Rennie and his dad come back Sunday night, it's finally finished.

"My dad's taking me to New England this summer," Rennie exclaims as he bursts into the bedroom. "Just him and me. It's going to be so neat. We're going to drive all over New England. Go camping up in Maine for a whole week."

George nods. He wouldn't mind having a dad like that himself. But he knows he's not supposed to say things like that. "What do you think?" he asks, pointing to the shadow box.

"Cool," Rennie says, but he barely gives it a glance. "Did I tell you there's a lake for canoes and kayaks at the camp in Maine?"

George waits till Rennie goes downstairs before he picks up the phone and dials. He's had his eye on it all evening, but he's not about to call when someone's around. It's Rennie's own private line, too.

He hears the phone ringing at the other end. Three, four, five times. He's about to hang up when he hears the *click*.

"Dad? Are you there?"

But it's not his dad's voice. It's just a recording. "The number you have dialed has been disconnected. The number you have dialed has been disconnected."

George hangs up. Dials again. He makes sure this time that he dials the correct numbers.

It rings. Again. And again. "The number you have dialed has been—"

George hangs up. He knows how the tape ends.

All of a sudden he grabs the shadow box. Clutching

it to his chest, he runs downstairs and out of the house. It's night now, and he can hear the crickets chirping away as he runs down the hill to the boathouse. When he reaches the river, he's panting hard.

"You're not going to throw your shadow box in the river too, are you, George?"

It's Brett. She sitting at the water's edge, arms around her knees.

"Too?" he asks. "What's that supposed to mean?"

"I saw you toss that baseball mitt in the river the first time you came here," Brett says. "For Rennie's birthday. Remember?"

Well, now he does, of course. Silently he turns and marches up the hill to the house, still clutching the shadow box to his chest.

Chapter Twenty-Three

WHEN GEORGE SHOWS up for school with his shadow box, it turns out half the class didn't even bother to do theirs. They're not being graded on it, so why bother? Some of the projects look like kids did them in their sleep, or had their sisters and brothers in kindergarten do the shadow boxes for them. Miles Chen glued two Indians passes and his old catcher's mitt to the back of his shadow box, and that was it. Even for Miles, that is low, George thinks. Except for Norman, who did paper dolls, most of the boys did sports. There are three other baseball boxes, two hockey, one basketball.

Miss Lemon puts the shadow boxes on the chalk tray under the blackboard. She asks the kids to come up, in groups of three and four, to check out the work.

"Pretend you're at an art gallery," she says. "It's opening night."

The kids act like they're being sent to detention. Once they're on their feet, however, George can tell some of them seem to like what they see. Rennie's is a big hit.

Fern's, he has to admit, is good too. She's done a theater, with a velvet curtain and half a dozen Christmas tree lights at the bottom to look like footlights. They light up, too. When you roll up the curtain, though, the show is over. A Barbie doll, dressed like a ballerina, is taking a bow.

"Is that supposed to be you, Fern?" Rennie asks.

"Yes." Fern beams. "It's so realistic, my mom says you can almost hear all the applause for me."

"If it were really real, there wouldn't be any applause," Rennie jokes.

The next one is called *The Lizard Who Ate East Siena*. It's got a toy lizard—scales, a tail, plus bulging eyes— towering over the town. When George checks it out, he even recognizes some of the local buildings, including the mill, with a yellow river running beside it.

"How did you do it?" Miss Lemon asks.

"The town was the easy part," Lizard explains. "I cut up some old picture postcards and glued them to matchboxes. Making the lizard was hard. I took apart an old teddy bear and covered it with leather I cut off a car seat at the recycling center. Then I glued on little bits of tin cans that I cut out with wire clippers. That made the scales. And the eyes are a golf ball cut in half to look all bulgy."

With that, Lizard makes her own eyes bulge out even farther than normal, and Fern lets out a scream that maybe isn't acting.

George's own shadow box gets almost as much attention, though. Most of the girls ignore it. All of the boys open the hood and lean in real close to check out the details underneath.

"Very cool," the boys say. "How did you do it?"

George explains how he recycled everything from the dump, but they don't care. Lizard listens in, though. But she doesn't say anything to him, and he doesn't say anything to her about her lizard.

At the end of the afternoon Miss Lemon gives out the awards. Lizard wins the People's Choice award because hers is the most popular. For a moment she is the most popular kid in class, too. Miss Lemon gives George a blue ribbon for Most Artistic.

He can hardly believe it. "But it's not pretty."

"Art doesn't have to be pretty," Miss Lemon explains. "It just has to be beautiful. Didn't I tell you that last time?"

George remembers, but he still has no idea what the heck Miss Lemon is talking about. Her brother has that used-car lot, he recalls. That probably explains it. Even so, he's proud. It's not every day he gets to feel good about something that's all his!

When the bell rings, the kids collect their shadow boxes.

"You did a good job with that engine, George," Lizard tells him.

"Thanks, Lizard."

"Well, don't you think I did a good job too? The kids loved it. Not just Miss Lemon. Rennie told me he liked it best."

"It's a neat shadow box, Lizard, but—"

"But what?"

"Did you have to make fun of yourself like that?" George asks. "Everybody was laughing at you. Didn't you even notice?"

Lizard shrugs it off. "I know I'm weird," she tells him. "I don't care what everyone says about me. I don't even mind what the kids say about people who live in trailer parks. Which is more than we can say about someone we both know."

"You talking about me?"

"Oh, George. Why don't you come back where you belong? With real people? Do you really need some butler to drive you around?"

"Oh, you don't know anything, Lizard. Rich people

are real. Besides, the butler doesn't drive. We've got a chauffeur to do that."

Lizard shakes her head.

"What?" he asks impatiently. "What are you looking like that for?"

"*We* got a chauffeur?" she asks, laughing a little. "You better be careful, George. It sounds like you're one fry short of a Happy Meal!"

"You're jealous. That's got to be it. You just wish you were up on Heights Road with the Whitfields too."

He clutches his shadow box to his chest and walks down the hall alone.

Rennie is waiting out front. So is the Mercedes with Murdoch at the wheel.

"I got another dentist appointment," he says. "You want to come along for the ride?"

George shakes his head. "I'll catch the bus, thanks," he says.

"Bet you can't wait to show Ga your blue ribbon," Rennie says. "She's going to be real impressed."

"With the ribbon maybe," George says. "She's not too big on engines."

Chapter Twenty-Four

GEORGE SITS BY himself, the shadow box on his lap, stroking the blue ribbon clipped to the top of it. He doesn't look up until the bus stops at the Whitfields'.

As he walks along the gravel to the main house he looks across the meadow. He can see Brett leading the horse around the corral. Brett and Rennie's mom is due back at the end of the week. Their dad is going in a couple days. Seems like their parents see even less of each other than they see of their kids.

George walks up to the front door. Thanks to him, they have started to lock it. But he's got a key now. He unlocks the door, steps into the foyer. Every time he sees that black-and-white marble, he remembers how cold it was the first time he dropped in.

George looks up. Mrs. Whitfield is at the top of the

stairs. Stiff hair as usual. All made up as usual. Today it's a green suit with a big gold pin on one lapel.

"George? Is that a blue ribbon I see? What's it for? Come show me!"

"No big deal," George says instinctively, clutching the box more tightly.

"Nonsense!" Mrs. Whitfield scoffs. "Blue ribbons are a very big deal!"

"It's just for this shadow box," he explains. "It's just a dumb project for school. A lot of kids did them."

"Rennie, too?"

"Oh, he did a great one," George tells her. "He did the motorboat. He made it look like it was flying out of the box. The kids really liked it."

"But you won first prize," Mrs. Whitfield says. "So someone liked yours even more."

"I suppose," George says.

She takes him by the elbow and leads him down the stairs and into the living room. Standing by the French doors, where the light is strongest, she takes the shadow box, lays it on the chess table.

"You're not going to like it," he warns her.

"Why not?" Mrs. Whitfield asks. "You don't like my taste in art?"

"It's dumb. It's an engine. You know, really common. I made it out of junk, and that's just what it looks like."

But she isn't listening to him. She's got the shadow box on her lap, and she's pulling the little medallion on the hood. "Oh, my!"

"I told you it was junk."

"How remarkable!" she exclaims.

"You like it?" he asks cautiously.

"I adore it! Even if you're not into engines, this one is something else. All of it recycled, you say?"

George nods. "You like it? Honest?"

"It's enchanting, George. Oh, there's no doubt about it. You've got a natural talent. It's a bit like a very famous art museum in Paris, George. All made out of pipes and twisted metal. Quite artistic. Why don't we drive down to the art store in town?"

"Now?"

"Oh, absolutely! We'll get you new paints, and brushes. An easel, of course. And some canvases. Oh, you'll need lots of art supplies, George. With some lessons, you could do real art."

"Miss Lemon says this is real art," George reminds her. "Most Artistic. That's what she says mine is. Most Artistic."

But Mrs. Whitfield is too engrossed in what she's thinking to hear what George is saying. "I could get Mr. Winslow from the academy," she says. "He'd be just the one for the job. He's expensive, but worth it, George. Would you like that, George?"

"It sounds like snails," George says, shrugging.

"Snails?"

"Oh, nothing," George sighs.

"To think I offered you every kind of lesson except art!" she exclaims. "I had no idea you were so talented, George. But I always said you were exceptional, didn't I? In a few months we could have you doing lovely landscapes, maybe even a portrait or two. Wouldn't that be something, George? Someday you could paint a young girl, just as someone painted me so long ago, George."

She pauses, looks up at the painting above the fireplace.

"You looked beautiful, Mrs. Whitfield."

"I mean the painting, George. Do you see the way the artist filled it with life, with movement, even though I seem to be sitting very, very still?"

"I can't."

"Oh, please, George. Of course you can't. Not yet. That's just the point. But you could! With the proper guidance. And you're going to get plenty of that, I can assure you."

"I can't have you doing more for me," he says. "It's not right, you doing all the giving and me doing all the taking."

"But it's my pleasure, George. Won't you let me recycle you, George?" Mrs. Whitfield says. "Let me make you into something special. Let me recycle you into an artist!"

"The way I recycled the trash into art?"

"Why, yes, George. Exactly."

"Most things just get recycled into the same stuff they were before," George says slowly, thoughtfully. "Newspapers get recycled into more newspapers. Tires get to be tires all over again. I guess a Coke can might end up as a Pepsi can. But it's still a can, Mrs. Whitfield."

"You're not trash," Mrs. Whitfield assures him. "It's not your fault who your family are, George."

"My family?" he asks. "What do they have to do with it?"

"A sister who couldn't care less," Mrs. Whitfield goes on. "God only knows what happened to your father. You deserve better than that, George."

"They got troubles," George explains. "That's why they're not here. It's not their fault or anything."

"Oh, George, be sensible," Mrs. Whitfield protests. "Even if they were here, they couldn't give you what you need."

"Lessons, you mean?"

"For starters," Mrs. Whitfield says.

"Clothes?"

"There's nothing wrong with dressing well, is there?"

"Nothing wrong that I can think of," he says.

"Come, sit next to me, George," says Mrs. Whitfield

as she leads him to the sofa. She sits and pats the seat next to her. "It's time we had a little talk."

"Have I done something wrong, Mrs. Whitfield?"

"Oh, no, George. Quite the opposite. You've done everything very well. You are getting to fit in so well. Why, you're almost a member of the family, George. In fact, I want to make that official."

"Official?"

"I want to adopt you, George! Make you into a fine young man. A Whitfield!"

"But I'm not an orphan. I got a dad. He's going to send for me real soon. I know he is."

"You could still visit him, of course, George. But you'd live here with us permanently. Surely you'd like that, wouldn't you?"

He picks up the shadow box. He hugs it to his chest. He starts up the stairs.

"George?"

He turns. Old Mrs. Whitfield is standing at the bottom of the stairs, one elegant hand on the banister where it curves. "Yes?"

"I said something wrong," she says. "I didn't mean what I—"

"But you did mean it," he says.

She nods. "But I never meant to hurt you. It's the last thing I wanted. I love you, George. You know that, don't you?"

Nodding weakly, George turns away from her, and climbs up the rest of the steps.

The next morning, at breakfast, he tells the Whitfields that his sister called when they were out.

"She wants me to come," he explains. "Right away. Even before school is over."

"Isn't there something we can do to change her mind?" Brett asks.

"She wants me there when her baby is born," George says.

No one counters. Old Mrs. Whitfield just nods silently.

Chapter Twenty-Five

THE CANDY MAN is back. He's filling the vending machine with Snickers, Mounds, Milky Ways, Frito-Lay's. George recognizes him, of course. George can't help feeling surprised that the guy recognizes him, too.

"Where you going this time, kid?" he asks.

"Pittsfield," George says.

"For a kid, you really get around, don't you?"

George nods. "Just living the life," he explains.

Lizard, sitting next to him on the old wooden bench in the bus station, sighs. "What's that supposed to mean?" she asks.

George shrugs. "It's conversation," he tells her. "It doesn't have to mean anything."

"Well, what's the point of talking if you don't—"

"You know, you don't have to wait with me," he

interrupts. "I can get on a bus all by myself, you know," he tells her.

"Actually, George, that's not something anybody knows," Lizard teases. "I'm here to make sure history doesn't repeat itself."

"If you have to stay, could you at least put a lid on it?"

"I suppose," she says sourly. "But if I'd stayed last time, you'd have spared yourself a lot of grief."

George shrugs. How is he supposed to explain to her that the Whitfields aren't bad or wrong or anything like that? It would be as hard as explaining Lizard to the Whitfields.

Life's hard enough already, and it looks like it's about to get harder once he gets to Pittsfield and explains to Tammy what he's doing there out of the blue.

Murdoch drove him to the bus station that morning. Rennie was off sailing with his dad. Brett had gone to some environmental meeting. Mrs. Whitfield walked him to the car, though. She even kissed him on the cheek. If she didn't believe him about Tammy calling, she never showed it. All she showed was how sad she was. That was hard enough. She stood on the front steps waving her hand at him.

He pulls a sheet of paper from his pocket. It's got the phone number of Tammy and Karl's neighbor.

"Bus for Pittsfield, Erie, Buffalo, now boarding at

gate eleven!" It's over the P.A. Scratchy but George can hear it all right.

"Now?" Lizard asks.

"I guess," George says.

He's dragging one duffel bag with one hand. She's dragging the other. The bike's in the middle. They've each got their free hand on the handlebars as they steer it to the gate.

"You need some help?"

It's a man's voice. George hears him, but he's got too much going on to turn back to look. "It's okay," George says. "I got enough time to get it on the bus by myself."

"Excuse me, son." The voice sounds very familiar.

"What the ..." George stops.

He lets go of the handlebar. He lets go of the strap on the duffel. He doesn't know how, or why or why not, but it doesn't matter. "Dad?" he gasps as he spins around on his heel.

But the man doesn't look anything like George's dad. Right away George feels like a complete and total jerk. Quickly, he grabs the strap to the duffel bag, slips it over his shoulder. He returns the other hand to the handlebar.

"You forget your dad is up in Canada scouting out oil wells?" Lizard asks.

"But it could be him," George tells her. "Not today. But some other time, it could be him."

"You believe that, George?" she says. "Really?"

"Of course I believe it," he tells her.

"Why, George?"

"Because I got no choice, Lizard," he tells her as he takes another step toward the waiting bus. "Some things a person's just got to believe. You know what I mean, Lizard?"

But he doesn't wait for her to reply. There isn't time. The bus is about to roll.